SHADOWS

OF THE

PAST

BOOKS BY:
JENNY ELAINE

Rose of Savannah Series

The Healing Rose of Savannah
The Whispering Shadows of Savannah

A Shady Pines Mystery Series

Secrets from the Past
Lost in the Past
Storms of the Past
Shadows of the Past

SHADOWS
OF THE
PAST

Jenny Elaine

PROLOGUE

Thunder rumbled in the distance as ten-year-old best friends, Mason and Lucas, raced through the woods behind Mason's house. The beam from their flashlight illuminated the many twigs and fallen branches that covered the forest floor, and they deftly leaped over a large log that lay in their path. The night was dark, and as a storm was brewing on the horizon and steadily drawing closer, neither the crickets nor the frogs were chirping.

"If my parents find out about this, I'll be dead," Lucas said in a breathless voice as he struggled to keep up with his friend.

"They won't find out," Mason assured him.

The two boys made it to the edge of the woods and stopped, both out of breath as they stared across the open field that stretched out before them. There, in the midst of the tall grass and weeds that dotted the otherwise barren landscape, a huge, abandoned building rose up before them like a relic from the past. Some of the windows were broken, vines slithered up the bones of the exterior like snakes, and rotted window shutters flapped lifelessly in the wind.

"Are you *sure* Adrian knew what he was talking about when he said this place was haunted?" Lucas asked in a shaky whisper.

Mason nodded and took a step forward, looking back at his friend questioningly when he didn't follow. "Aren't you coming?" he wanted to know.

Lucas hung back, his eyes wary as he stared at the building. "I-I think I'll just stay here," he stammered. "You go on ahead."

Pursing his lips in annoyance, Mason reached back and grabbed his friend by the arm. "What is *wrong* with you? Don't you want the chance to see a *real* ghost?" His eyes narrowing, Mason added, "Or are you scared?"

Lucas cleared his throat and stood up straighter. "N-no. Not if you aren't," he stated bravely.

"Well, come on then."

Still clutching his friend by the arm, Mason all but dragged Lucas across the field toward the supposedly haunted building that loomed larger and larger the closer they got. Just then, a bolt of lightning streaked across the sky above their heads, and Lucas shivered as the wind whistled around the building and through the trees behind them. It sounded almost like a ghost in itself, the way it moaned and whined like a lost soul in torment.

They finally reached the building, a place that every kid's parent in town forbade them to visit, and they stared up at the old structure in awe. It was even bigger up close, and the stories told about this place were enough to give a kid nightmares. Was it really haunted, though? That's what they'd come to find out. Or, at least, Mason wanted to find out. Lucas, on the other hand, only came along because his friend had a knack for talking him into things.

Suddenly, the moaning of the wind grew louder, and what sounded like the breaking of glass shattered the otherwise stillness of their surroundings. Both boys gasped at the sudden sound, but neither was prepared for what happened next. A flash of lightning lit up the black sky, and in one of the smudged, second-story windows, there appeared the face of a woman. She was deathly pale with a taunt face surrounded by ash-colored curls, and she stared down at the boys with a look of utter agony in her eyes. She opened her mouth in what appeared to be a muted scream, just as a mighty clap of thunder shook the ground beneath the boys' feet. Then, just as quickly as she'd appeared, she was gone.

Spinning on their heels, Mason and Lucas raced back across the field as quickly as their trembling legs would carry them. What they didn't know, however, was that now another face stared out from that same window, watching their retreating figures with a menacing glare.

CHAPTER 1

5 DAYS BEFORE

"Pops?"

As Tori walked through the darkened hardware store toward the back room, she wondered why her grandfather had sent that strange text, asking her to come by the store to help him with something. He normally wasn't big on texting, but she hadn't thought much about it. Until now. Now that she was here and the store was so empty and quiet, she felt like something might be wrong.

"Pops, it's Tori. Are you here?" she tried again.

When he didn't answer her, she felt a strong sense of foreboding as she pushed open the door that led into the back room and her grandfather's office. Something wasn't right, but as soon as she spotted Pops lying on the floor with an oozing cut on his head, all caution was thrown aside.

She'd barely gone two steps when a rag soaked in chloroform was pressed over her mouth and nose, and Tori felt panic shoot through her veins. She fought against the strong arms that held her tightly, but there was no use. She slowly slipped into unconsciousness and slumped lifelessly to the floor.

There was a heaviness weighing on Tori's chest as she slowly began to awaken. The room was dark and the air felt so thick that for one terrifying moment, she felt like she couldn't breathe. Her heart rate quickened as a cold chill swept across her skin. Blinking her eyes, she wondered why she couldn't see anything, and also why she felt so sick to her stomach.

Taking a slow, deep breath in through her mouth, Tori tried to reach a hand up to her face, only to realize both her hands were tied behind her back. It seemed she was sitting in a metal chair inside a cold, dark, and unfamiliar room. With a moan, she began struggling against the ties that had her bound, feeling pricks of panic shooting through her body like fiery darts.

Suddenly, a bright light clicked on just above her head, and she jerked in surprise. The spotlight was so intense that she had to close her eyes for a moment against its blinding beam. She felt confused and disoriented, and although she was freezing cold, her skin was sweaty and clammy.

"It's about time you woke up."

Tori's eyes popped open just as a quick inhale of breath passed her lips. The voice had come from her right, and she jerked her gaze in that direction, searching the shadows.

"Don't bother," he said. "You can't see me."

Trembling all over, Tori swallowed past what

felt like sandpaper in her throat and asked, "Wh-who are you?"

"Does it matter? I don't think it does."

Tori tried to remember what had happened, her mind so muddled that she was having a difficult time deciphering between reality and imagination. The last thing she remembered was going over to the hardware store after receiving a text from Pops. What happened after that?

"You look a little confused."

The voice was low and the tone cynical. She could feel his eyes boring into her, and she pushed herself further back against the chair. Why was he keeping himself hidden? She just couldn't seem to understand…

Suddenly, it all came flooding back. When she'd gone to the store, she'd found Pops lying in the back room with a bloody gash on his head. Before she could react, however, someone had sneaked up behind her with a chloroform-soaked rag.

"Julian Cooper?" she whispered in horror.

Panic threatened to overtake her as memories of that horrible night when her oven repairman, Julian Cooper, tried to attack her. At least, she'd *thought* it was Cooper, but she couldn't be certain because she'd never actually seen his face. She'd gone to Misty Raven's house to let her dog out when the lights had suddenly shut off. She could still see his shadowy silhouette as he lunged across the kitchen toward her…

She was beginning to hyperventilate. Her heart

was pounding so heavily that her chest hurt. She needed to put her head between her knees, but with her hands bound, she could barely move.

"You should really calm down, Miss Barlow. It's not good to get so upset."

Fighting to control herself before she totally lost it, Tori took a deep breath and asked in a fearful tone, "Why have you done this? What are you going to do with me?"

He didn't immediately respond, and Tori wanted to scream at him through the thick silence. After a moment, he chuckled lightly and said in a singsong voice, "You'll find out soon enough."

CHAPTER 2

Misty
Monday evening

Misty rode with Brice to the hardware store, her fingernails digging into her palms as her stomach twisted with fear. Brice's own hands clutched the steering wheel so hard they were turning white, and Misty knew he was just as upset as she was. Tori had been kidnapped? She couldn't believe it. The statistics of a missing person ever being found kept going over and over in her mind, and she knew the first twenty-four hours were the most crucial. What if they couldn't find her in time?

The sun was starting to set, casting shadows all around the silent town of Shady Pines as they drove down Main Street. The flashing lights of police cars and an ambulance could be seen up ahead at Barlow's Hardware Store, and as they passed Tori's little coffee shop, Misty felt tears prick the back of her eyes. Tori was like a sister, and it killed her to think of what her sweet friend must be going through right now.

With squealing tires, Brice turned into the store's parking lot and pulled around to the back. He and Misty jumped from his truck and hurried inside, where they found several police officers, Tori's mom, and a paramedic tending to Tori's and Brice's grandfather.

"Pops, are you okay?" Brice asked as he rushed to his grandfather's side.

"He refuses to go to the hospital," the paramedic stated matter-of-factly before Pops could answer. "So, I'm stitching him up here. He has a mild concussion, so he'll need to take it easy for the next couple of days."

"I don't have time to take it easy," Pops said, his voice trembling. "I've got to help find my girl."

Misty immediately went to Amy Barlow's side and wrapped a supportive arm around the older woman's shoulders. Tori's dad, Neil, was still in the hospital after having a bad car wreck, and Amy was so pale that she looked to be on the verge of hysteria.

"Do you know what happened?" Misty gently asked as she slowly looked around. The police were thoroughly combing the back room of the store, but nothing seemed to be out of order. The only thing unusual that Misty noticed was a bloodstain on the floor, which she suspected came from Mr. Barlow's head wound.

Amy shook her head. "No," she replied, reaching up to wipe her eyes. "All I know is that I received an odd text from Tori, so I left Savannah and came to see what was going on. I found Pops lying on the floor; he'd just regained consciousness and was trying to get up."

Her brow furrowing, Misty asked, "What did the text say?"

With trembling hands, Amy unlocked her cell phone and showed the message to Misty.

"Please come to the hardware store ASAP."

"I tried to call both her and Pops, but my calls went straight to voicemail," Amy said. Bursting into tears, she covered her face and said in a broken voice, "Why didn't I call Brice or even the police instead of coming myself? They would have gotten here sooner and might have prevented this."

Patting Amy on the back, Misty said, "Don't blame yourself, Mrs. Amy. I have a feeling the kidnapper sent that text from Tori's phone after he'd already taken her."

What Misty couldn't figure out, though, was **why** he'd sent it. Why would he want to call immediate attention to Tori's kidnapping? It didn't make sense.

As Misty and Mrs. Amy stood together in an out-of-the-way corner while the police searched the room for evidence, Misty slowly took everything in. The new sheriff in town, Sheriff Ward, was in charge and loudly giving orders. He was in his late fifties, with white hair and a mustache. Originally from Shady Pines, he'd moved to Statesboro with his wife when they were first married. After her death, he heard that Shady Pines needed a new sheriff and decided to come back home and apply for the job. He'd owned and operated a martial arts studio in Statesboro for over thirty years, and the citizens of Shady Pines felt he was more than qualified for the job of sheriff. Misty barely knew the man, but from what she'd observed, he was very stern and an obsessive perfectionist.

Then there was Detective Dylan Mitchell. He'd moved to Shady Pines a few months before Misty. He was in his early thirties, and even though Misty had held several conversations with the man, she hardly knew anything about him. From what she'd heard, he'd spent several years in the military before coming to Shady Pines. He was handsome and quiet, but from what she'd seen of him in the past, he was very thorough and good at his job, and she trusted him to do his best to find Tori.

And lastly, her eyes moved over to the town's new rookie cop, Harris Hamilton. He'd moved to Shady Pines a couple of months ago and looked to be only about twenty-one or two. He was tall and slender, with a shy and somewhat awkward disposition, and he wore a pair of large glasses that constantly slid down his nose. According to the rumor mill, he'd applied at the Chatham County Police Department first but was turned down, so he came here.

Just then, Sheriff Ward and Dylan Mitchell came over to speak to Mrs. Amy, and Misty felt the older woman's fingers tighten around her arm. Pops brushed the paramedic's hand away and, with Brice's help, joined the others to hear what was being said.

"Amy," Sheriff Ward began, "after learning that

the kidnapper was already in the back room when Mr. Barlow entered, we checked for any signs of forced entry, but couldn't find any. We think maybe he slipped inside when Mr. Barlow took out the trash and then hid himself in the restroom until everyone was gone and the store was closed. Since Mr. Barlow's truck is missing, we believe the kidnapper stole it."

Sheriff Ward paused to slide on a pair of reading glasses so he could better see the notes he'd written. "Unfortunately, Mr. Barlow doesn't have security cameras outside," he continued. "We plan to ask around town tomorrow morning in the hope that someone saw something. We're also dusting for fingerprints, but I don't think we'll find any. Right now, our main hope is to find an eyewitness. We'll also put an APB out on Mr. Barlow's truck."

"Pops always parks his truck out back, and the back door faces nothing but woods," Amy said, her eyes filling with tears. "If he took Tori out that way, I doubt anyone saw him."

Especially this late in the evening, Misty thought, but didn't dare say it out loud. She hoped the stereotypical small town filled with nosy people would come in handy this once.

"What if no one saw anything?" Brice wanted to know. "What then?"

Sheriff Ward hesitated, and Misty's stomach clenched. It seemed they didn't have much to go on, and that frightened her even more.

"Maybe we'll find some fingerprints after all," he finally replied in a hopeful tone. "We can also check the camera out on Main Street; perhaps it caught something. Also, Dylan and Harris and a couple of others are about to look through those woods out back. If he came through that bog to get here, then there's bound to be footprints."

"Do you think Julian Cooper is the culprit?" Misty asked, finally voicing the question that had been weighing heavily on her mind since she first heard Tori was kidnapped.

Sheriff Ward shook his head. "I don't know, Miss Raven. My first instinct is to say yes, but we just can't be certain yet. We've been in contact with the Savannah police since Miss Barlow's attack last week, and Cooper hasn't been seen."

"Sheriff Ward?"

Everyone turned to see Harris holding up a torn piece of paper in a gloved hand.

"What is it, Harris?" Sheriff Ward asked.

Walking over to stand next to the sheriff, Harris handed him the paper and said, "I found this note shoved underneath the desk."

Everyone crowded in closer to peer at the typed note, which read: *"You have until Monday to find what's been taken. That's only 7 days, so don't be mistaken."*

Looking from the message to Pops and Brice, Sheriff Ward asked, "Did either of you write this?"

They both shook their heads, and Pops asked, "Do you think the kidnapper wrote it?"

"It would appear so," Sheriff Ward replied.

"It would also appear that our kidnapper likes to play games," Officer Dylan Mitchell muttered as he took the note and studied it.

"But what does the message mean?" Amy asked, her tone fearful. "Is...is he saying that next Monday he's going to...?"

Touching Mrs. Amy on the arm, Dylan said, "We can't know for certain what it means."

In a heavy tone, Brice stated, "I think we all know what it means, Dylan. If we don't act quickly, time is going to run out for Tori."

As Brice drove Misty home, the silence between them was heavy. All either of them could think about was Tori, and they both knew if the police didn't find her soon, they may never see her again.

Mrs. Amy had gone back to Savannah to see how soon her husband could return home. Mr. Neil's leg was in bad shape and he'd need a lot of rest and physical therapy, but Misty knew neither of them wanted to be nearly thirty minutes away during such a time. She couldn't imagine what they must be feeling; Tori was their only daughter, and the three of them were exceptionally close.

Brice turned down Misty's long, pine-shaded driveway, his truck bumping along the dirt road as they drew closer to her house. After he dropped her off, he planned to stay with Pops to make certain there would be no adverse effects from his head wound. Poor Pops. He felt responsible for Tori's kidnapping; Misty had heard him apologize to Mrs. Amy for letting it happen. It wasn't his fault, though. They all knew that. Misty was just thankful that Pops was okay.

The old Victorian-style home looked dark and lonely in the twilight of the evening as they drew closer, and the random thought that she'd soon need to have it painted drifted through Misty's mind. She'd been working so hard to get the renovations done on this place so she could open it as a B&B once again. If something happened to Tori, though, she wasn't certain she could remain in Shady Pines. It would just be too painful.

"Come on," Brice said as he parked the truck. "I'll walk you inside."

The woods surrounding Misty's house were eerily silent as she climbed from Brice's truck; not even the crickets were chirping. As they walked up the front porch steps, she wished she'd thought to leave a light on before they'd left earlier. Fumbling around in the darkness for her keys, Misty paused when she suddenly heard a rustling out in the bushes.

"Did you hear that?" she whispered.

Brice nodded, his eyes searching the shadows. "It must have been a raccoon or something," he said when the rustling stopped.

Misty sighed. "I guess my nerves are just on edge."

Brice turned to look back at her as she unlocked

the front door and swung it open. "You're more than welcome to stay with Pops and me, Misty. I don't want you to be frightened."

"I'll be fine," Misty said as she turned on the foyer lights. Her massive dog, Wally, barked loudly from the kitchen just then, and she added with a small, half smile, "I have a bodyguard, remember?"

Nodding, Brice ran his fingers through his thick, blonde hair and sighed. The look of worry over his cousin weighed so heavily on his face that Misty's heart clenched. Reaching out, she gently touched his arm and said softly, "They're going to find her, Brice. I know they will."

Brice stared at her for a moment in silence, his eyes filled with both hope and fear. He stepped forward then and pulled her into a hug, his arms warm as they encircled her. Feeling a little surprised by the sudden gesture but not at all against it, Misty rested her cheek against his chest and closed her eyes. She could feel the tension in his body and knew he needed the comfort of physical contact with someone he cared about. And Brice **did** care for her, she didn't doubt that. What his intentions were toward her, though, she couldn't say, nor did she care to have that particular discussion just yet. She and Brice needed each other right now, and that's all that mattered.

"I'll see you later, okay?" Brice said, pulling back. "Call me if you need anything."

Misty nodded and told him good night, closing

and locking the door behind him when he left. Feeling tired and worried and stressed, she went into the kitchen to see about Wally and to fix herself a hot cup of chamomile tea.

While the tea steeped, Misty sat at the kitchen table and rubbed Wally's ears, her body aching with weariness. It had been a long ten days. She and Brice had only just returned from Dahlonega the day before after an impromptu trip to find her father. The trip had been quite eventful, to say the least, and now she was faced with yet another crisis.

It wasn't until that very moment that Misty remembered the email from the DNA website she'd just recently joined. She'd been about to read the results when Brice came bursting in with the news about Tori. Glancing at her cell phone as it rested quietly on the kitchen table, she chewed her bottom lip in thought. Inside that phone was the answer she'd been searching for all these years. Was she ready to know who her birth father was?

Misty reached for her phone but then paused, withdrawing her hand quickly back to her side. She wasn't prepared to deal with that right now. Once they found Tori and she knew everything was okay, then she'd read the results.

CHAPTER 3

Tuesday morning

The sun was just beginning to creep its way into the sky when Misty walked out with Wally. She'd barely slept all night for worrying about Tori. She wanted to do something to help but knew she would have to be careful not to interfere with the police investigation. She'd had her hand slapped many times before for doing just that, and she wasn't certain she wanted to cross the stern Sheriff Ward. She **had** to do something, though. She couldn't just sit idly by while her best friend was at the mercy of a psychopath.

The morning was dark and still, with no sign of life anywhere about. Wally sniffed quietly around the yard, the crunching of twigs and dead leaves beneath his massive paws the only sound that filled the silence. With a yawn, Misty wrapped her sweater-clad arms around her waist and warded off a chill. It was the last week of April and surprisingly still quite cool in the mornings, but Misty was used to the unpredictable weather in the southeast.

Once Wally was finished outside, the two went back inside for breakfast. Misty had just grabbed

Wally's food bowl when he suddenly let out a ferocious bark and bounded through the house toward the front door. Her brow furrowing, Misty hurried after him, wondering what he'd heard.

The house was dark and their footsteps echoed loudly off the bare floors. Wally stopped at the front door and barked again, his tail down and ears back. Since it was still pretty dark outside, Misty flipped on the front porch light and waited for a second, thinking maybe a wild animal was on the porch. When Wally continued to growl and bark, Misty attached the safety chain to the door and slowly cracked it open.

"Is anyone there?" she called out through the tiny opening.

No one answered, and just before she shut the door, something resting on the mat caught Misty's eye. After removing the chain, she opened the door further and picked up one single red rose and a folded-up piece of paper.

"Wally, come back inside," she commanded her dog when he started to run out into the front yard. Apparently, someone had just been on her porch, and since she hadn't heard the sound of a vehicle, she suspected they didn't wish to be discovered.

Following her dog back inside the house, Misty locked the front door and flipped on the foyer light. She unfolded the note and began to read the unfamiliar handwriting: *"Misty, Misty, with hair as black as a raven's wings and eyes the color of silver. You never see me, but I see you, and I long to hold you forever."*

Blinking in surprise, Misty stood there for a moment in confusion. Who would come to her house so early in the morning and leave a rose and what appeared to be a love note at her front door?

Retrieving her phone, Misty texted a picture of the note to Dylan Mitchell. There was something very strange about the whole thing. It was apparently meant to be some sort of flirtation, but it made her feel uneasy.

"It seems you have a secret admirer," was Dylan's response. *"Brice or Adam, maybe?"*

"No," she replied. *"Neither of them would do something like this. It's too creepy. Plus, I don't recognize the handwriting."*

"If you're concerned about it, put the note in a plastic bag and I'll send someone out later to pick it up," he told her. *"It will be a little while, though, before I can look into it. We are pretty wrapped up with this kidnapping case right now."*

"Oh, I totally understand," Misty immediately responded. *"Did y'all find anything in the woods behind the hardware store?"*

It took several minutes for Dylan to reply, and when he finally did, the text read, *"Yes, a shoe print. We made a cast of it and plan to go back for it later this morning."*

"That's good news," Misty replied. *"Keep me updated?"*

"Sure thing."

Putting the phone into her robe pocket, Misty

went into the kitchen to grab a bag for the note. As she carefully placed the note inside, she wondered yet again who would do such a thing. Perhaps Dylan would be able to lift some fingerprints from it; if her own hadn't smudged them, that is.

After giving Wally his breakfast, Misty decided to go back to the hardware store and have a look around. The police were finished searching the place, after all, so what could it hurt? She quickly changed her clothes and grabbed a banana on the way out. The thought that it might not be the safest idea to go to the store by herself crossed her mind, but she pushed it away. The whole town would be waking up soon, so it shouldn't be too dangerous.

Tori

The sound of the key turning in the lock echoed loudly throughout the bare room. Tori jerked her head in that direction and watched as the door swung open to reveal the large silhouette of a man. He held something in his hand; it looked like a glass, and she hoped it was something to drink.

"Sleep well?"

The voice sent chills down Tori's spine. He'd left her alone in this dark room all night with nothing to drink and no bed upon which to sleep. She was hungry and chilled to the bone, but at least he'd finally untied her. She'd paced about the room all night, feeling around for a way of escape but finding none. The room didn't even have a window, and she couldn't help but wonder where he was keeping her. The building was obviously quite old; it creaked and groaned with the wind as if it might tumble to the ground at any moment. From what she could tell now in the dim lighting, however, was that the door and lock looked new, which let Tori know he'd made certain it wouldn't be easy for her to escape.

"Why are you doing this?" she asked, on the verge of tears.

Stuffing the key to the deadbolt inside his pocket, he stepped into the room and shut the door behind him. He then clicked on a small flashlight and shone it into her face.

"You didn't answer my question," he stated.

Tori blinked and looked away from the bright light. Rubbing her arms as she stepped away from him, she said, "No, I didn't sleep well. How could I? You didn't even give me a blanket."

"How thoughtless of me," he replied cynically. "I'll be sure to bring you one later, along with your lunch. Right now, I have to get to work, but I'll return soon."

He carefully placed the glass on the floor, and as he walked back toward the door, Tori took a tentative step forward. Her mind was screaming at her to escape while the door was unlocked, but could she catch him off guard and manage to get past him? If he'd left the chair, she could have hit him with it, but he'd removed it the night before and she had no weapon. Thoughts of the self-defense training Officer Dylan Mitchell had given her shot through her mind, but before she could make a move, he spun around and shone the light back into her eyes.

"I wouldn't try anything if I were you, Miss Barlow," he stated calmly, but she could clearly hear the threat in his voice. "If you behave, I might go easier on you. If you try to escape, though, something terrible might happen to your family. Your grandfather may suffer another blow to the head, or worse, and your parents might have another wreck."

Tori gasped, her blood running cold. "So, you really **were** responsible for their car accident?" she rasped, her whole body beginning to tremble.

He laughed then, and the deep, guttural sound sent chills down the back of Tori's neck. "You ask far too many questions, Miss Barlow."

With that, he walked out and slammed the door behind him. The sound of the deadbolt clicking into place gave Tori the feeling of finality, as if she would remain in this cold prison cell for the rest of her life. Choking back a sob, she pressed her back against the wall and slowly sank to the floor as tears began to flow silently down her cheeks.

CHAPTER 4

Misty

Misty pulled into the hardware store's parking lot and drove around to the back. The morning was still quite dark as a group of gray clouds covered up the sun, and as Misty climbed from her car and walked toward the back door, she felt a shiver run down her spine. Seeing the police tape scattered around and just knowing what happened here made her feel tense and uneasy.

After finding the hidden key in the spot where Brice had once shown Misty, she used it to open the back door and stepped inside. The room was dark and still, and for a moment, Misty simply stood there and allowed her gaze to scan the room. She pictured Tori walking in from the front, her face filling with horror when she spotted Pops lying on the floor. The kidnapper must have been waiting behind the door and grabbed Tori as soon as she rushed further into the room to help her grandfather.

Her eyes moving over to where Pops had fallen, Misty wondered with what the kidnapper had used to strike him. Had he taken the weapon with him, or perhaps wiped it clean and put it back in its place within the room? She noted the many objects resting about that could have been used: a fishing trophy, a hammer, a paperweight. She supposed the police had dusted everything and found no fingerprints, but what if they'd missed something?

After carefully walking around the room and peering into every nook and cranny she could find, Misty finally gave up and went back outside. Facing the trees that rested only a few yards from the back door, she suddenly wondered what was on the other side of those woods. Not knowing how to get there by car, she once again allowed her curiosity to get the better of her. After grabbing a flashlight from her glove compartment, she stuffed her phone and car keys into her back pocket and headed into the dark, shadowy abyss.

As Misty entered further into the thick undergrowth, it felt like she was stepping into another world. The woods were dense and dark, and not a sound could be heard other than the crunching of her footsteps. No chirping of birds or the scurrying of squirrels was audible among the trees and bushes. It was like these woods had been abandoned by all living things, and Misty immediately felt a chill raise the hair on her arms.

The ground was moist and boggy, and Misty soon began to wish she'd worn rain boots. She couldn't imagine how the police had managed to find any evidence in this muck, and she began to regret her sudden decision to take this little trek. Something about these woods was oppressing, like a thick heaviness hung amongst the tops of the trees, watching her with hard, beady eyes.

Suddenly, a rustling in the leaves caught Misty's attention, and when she looked down, a large black snake was only inches away from her foot. With a yelp, she quickly jumped backward and slammed into a tree with a painful *thud*. The tree's limbs shook above her head and leaves scattered to the forest floor as the snake slithered away. With a shiver, Misty made sure to go in the opposite direction. Poisonous or not, she was absolutely terrified of snakes.

She walked for another fifteen minutes before finally reaching an opening. With a sigh of relief, she stepped from the woods and into a small clearing. She stopped and slowly looked around, her eyes widening when they landed on something just across the way. There, nestled among the trees, was Pops' truck.

Misty stood very still and quiet, her ears tuned to her surroundings. Was the kidnapper close by, or had he simply dumped the truck here and left? There was no sign of life or movement anywhere about; in fact, the area was quite desolate. The grass, however, appeared to have recently been mowed, and Misty spotted a tree stand just up ahead. Apparently, this was a popular hunting spot, but Misty had no idea who owned the property.

Slowly, Misty made her way over to the truck. Careful not to touch anything, she peered through the windows to find that the vehicle was empty. Could this be where the kidnapper had left his car before hiking through the woods to the store? He then would have driven away with Tori in Pops' truck and switched vehicles here in these woods. What Misty couldn't figure out, though, was why Dylan and the other officers hadn't found this already. Had they not walked all the way through the woods last night as she had just done?

Taking a photo of the truck, Misty texted it to Dylan. She'd planned to wait for him to call her, but when a sudden rustling in the trees behind the truck met her ears, she decided to head back to the store. Something about this place set her teeth on edge, and she wanted to get back to her car as quickly as possible.

Misty made her way back through the woods much more quickly this time. She had almost made it back to the store when the sound of footsteps suddenly met her ears. She stopped and peered through the few remaining trees ahead to see the large form of a man walking along the edge of the woods. The foliage was too thick to see who the man was, and Misty suddenly realized what a bad idea it had been to come here by herself. The store itself was on the edge of town, and since she was all the way at the back of the building, it was very probable that no one would hear her if she cried out for help. Had the kidnapper returned to the scene of the crime?

The man was drawing closer to where Misty

stood, and she quickly ducked behind the nearest tree. Her foot landed on a large twig, snapping it in half with a loud *crack.* Her heart catching, she peered around the tree to see that the man had stopped and seemed to be looking directly at her.

"Misty?"

When the familiar voice called out, Misty sighed in relief and stepped away from her hiding place.

"I'm here," she replied as she pushed her way through the remainder of the trees and bushes. When she emerged from the thick undergrowth, her shoes were covered in mud and her hair was a mess.

"Misty, what on earth are you doing?"

Adam Dawson stood before her, his eyes wide as he surveyed her disheveled appearance. Misty hadn't seen him since her return from Dahlonega, and she self-consciously tried to smooth her hair.

"I just wanted to have a look around," she stated matter-of-factly.

Adam raised his eyebrows, his black eyes staring piercingly at Misty. "And you thought coming out here by yourself so early in the morning when a kidnapper is on the loose was a good idea?" he asked.

"I guess I didn't really think it through," she muttered. Her eyes brightened, and she grabbed her phone from her pocket to show him the photo she'd taken. "Look at what I found, though. Pop Barlow's stolen truck was hidden on the other side of these woods."

As Adam took her phone to look at the picture, Misty looked back at the thick, dark trees and asked, "Who owns that property?"

Adam thought it over for a moment. "I think that's Mr. Porter's property. He has about twenty acres that he uses for hunting and fishing."

"So, he doesn't live somewhere near there?"

Adam shook his head. "No. He lives on the other side of town."

"Then that would be the perfect spot to leave a getaway car," she said. Tilting her head, she asked, "What are you doing out here, anyway?"

Running his fingers through his thick, black hair, Adam said, "I was driving by and spotted your car, so I thought I'd stop and see what was going on. I heard about Tori last night, so I figured you were here nosing around. How are you, Misty?"

Opening her car door to retrieve some wet wipes for her filthy hands, Misty said, "I'm okay; just worried sick about Tori."

She'd just finished wiping her hands when her phone started to ring.

"Misty, where are you?" Dylan asked as soon as she answered.

Misty told him and was about to ask why they hadn't discovered the truck themselves when he interrupted in a rather tense tone, "It was getting too dark for us to check out Mr. Porter's property last night, so we were going there later this morning when we went back for the mold of the shoe print. You really shouldn't be out there, Misty, nosing around like that. It's too dangerous."

"I'm sorry," she said, a little surprised that he seemed angry with her. "I was just trying to help." Hoping to change the subject, she cleared her throat and asked, "Have y'all tried tracing Tori's phone?"

"Yes, but apparently it's been turned off," he replied.

Misty sighed in frustration. "Do you think finding any video footage is a possibility?"

"I'm afraid not," he stated in a heavy tone. "From what I've seen this morning, the only camera on Main Street is in front of the bank, which is on the opposite side of town."

Misty's heart sank. "Have you talked to anyone yet?" she asked hopefully. "Maybe someone saw something."

"We plan to speak to everyone in town as soon as the stores start to open," he replied. "I stopped by the O'Reilly house a few minutes ago, and Catherine said she saw Mr. Barlow's truck driving away from the store last night, but it was too dark to see the driver. Their antique store is right down the street, you know, so I was really hopeful they saw something."

Before Misty could ask anything else, Dylan announced he was getting another call and their conversation was ended. With a sigh, she told Adam everything Dylan had said. As they talked, they slowly walked toward their vehicles.

"Who would do something like this, Adam?" she

asked as she opened her car door and tossed her phone onto the passenger seat.

Adam shook his head. "I don't know, but you need to be careful. I don't want you to be the next victim."

Misty leaned into her car and cranked it, glad that her back was toward him. After their kiss over two months ago, so much had happened and the two of them had simply drifted apart. She knew he cared about her, but she wasn't certain of her feelings for him. Her mind was too muddled to think about that right now, though, and she turned back to face him with a small smile.

"I'll be fine," she assured him.

With a nod, Adam glanced at his watch and said he had to get to work.

"I was supposed to be at Mrs. Neely's house ten minutes ago to wire her new patio," he told her. "Keep me updated?"

Misty promised she would, and after urging her to please be careful, Adam climbed into his truck and drove away. As Misty headed home to take a much needed shower, she thought again about Dylan's apparent irritation over her interference. She'd been involved with investigations around town before and he'd never seemed annoyed by it. So, why was he acting different this time?

CHAPTER 5

Tori

It hadn't even been twenty-four hours yet, and Tori felt like she was going crazy. She'd screamed and called out for help until her throat was raw, and then she'd paced around the dark room like a caged animal. Her mind kept whirling with questions about what he planned to do with her. Was he going to kill her, or just keep her here as a prisoner? Would he torture or abuse her? If so, she'd rather he just go ahead and kill her.

She was also sick with worry over Pops. When she'd last seen him, he was lying on the floor with a bloody gash on his head. Was he alright, or had this maniac killed him? And what of her parents? She knew they would be frantic with worry, and with everything they'd been through recently, they didn't need this added stress. She hated what was happening, and she was so tense and filled with fear that her body felt like a tightly wound-up cord.

The room was so dark that she couldn't tell what time of day it was, but when he returned with a tray of food, she assumed it to be around lunchtime.

"Hungry?" he asked, his voice echoing off the

bare walls. He held the tray in one hand, and a flashlight in the other.

"Yes," Tori replied softly. She was so weak from all the pacing and lack of food that she could barely push herself off the floor where she'd been sitting.

"I brought you this, too," he added, tossing a blanket at her.

Surprised, Tori caught the blanket and said, "Thank you."

"You sound a little hoarse," he stated. "Have you been calling out for help?"

Tori hesitated. "Y-yes," she finally replied, backing herself up against the far wall. What would he do to her for admitting the truth?

With a chuckle, he said, "There's really no need to strain your voice, Miss Barlow. No one can hear you."

"Where am I?" she asked, immediately regretting the question when she saw his silhouette stiffen.

He didn't immediately respond, but after a moment, his stance relaxed and he said, "You're in a place far away from everyone. They'll never find you here."

With that being said, he placed the tray and flashlight on the floor and left. Hurrying across the room, Tori sat down to eat what appeared to be a ham sandwich. He'd also brought a bottle of water, and she finished the meal in record time. For a moment, she felt her strength return, but it wasn't long before an extreme amount of fatigue flooded over her. What had he put in the sandwich to drug her? Was it poison? Should she try to vomit everything back up?

Before she could figure out what to do, the drug took effect and she slumped unconsciously to the floor.

Misty

Misty had just stepped out of the shower when her doorbell rang, and Wally's barks quickly began to echo throughout the house. With a sigh, she hurriedly tied her hair in a towel and slid into a bathrobe. When she opened the front door, she was surprised to see the new rookie cop, Harris, standing on her porch.

As soon as Harris saw that Misty was wearing a bathrobe, his face flushed with embarrassment and he cleared his throat awkwardly. "I, uh, was sent here by Officer Mitchell to retrieve the note that was left at your door this morning," he told her, barely meeting her gaze.

"Oh, sure," Misty replied, shoving Wally out of the way as she turned to grab the note off the foyer table. Handing it to Harris, she smiled and said, "Here you go. You know, Harris, I was pretty impressed when you discovered that note last evening left by the kidnapper."

Shuffling his feet, Harris glanced downward and said, "Thanks. I appreciate that. I'm just glad I didn't miss it and get yelled at by the sheriff like

Officer Mitchell."

Misty raised her eyebrows. "The sheriff yelled at Dylan?"

Harris nodded and pushed his glasses up his nose. "Yes, ma'am. The sheriff was furious that it was you instead of Officer Mitchell who found Mr. Barlow's truck. When he overheard him talking to you about it, he jumped on Officer Mitchell with all fours."

Misty frowned. "That's ridiculous," she said. "Did Dylan tell Sheriff Ward that he was planning to investigate that area this morning and I simply got there first?"

"Who knows?" Harris shrugged. "Officer Mitchell doesn't say much. Sheriff Ward says enough for the both of them; he can be pretty intimidating, you know."

Misty laughed. "I know what you mean."

Smiling shyly, Harris nodded to her and began to back away. "Thanks for the note, Miss Raven. I've got to get back to the station, but Officer Mitchell said to tell you he'll keep you updated."

Just as Misty said goodbye and shut the door, she heard her cell phone begin to ring. Hurrying back into the bathroom, she saw Brice's name flashing across the screen.

"Sorry I'm just now calling you back," Brice said when she answered, his tone weary. "I was helping Aunt Amy get Uncle Neil home."

"Oh, the hospital released him?" Misty asked in surprise.

"Yes, but other than physical therapy, he's pretty much bedridden," Brice stated. "He and Aunt Amy want to be home, though, instead of in Savannah right now."

"I can understand that," Misty replied. "How is Pops?"

"Neither of us slept much at all last night," Brice said with a yawn. "He seems to be doing fine, though, so I'm happy about that."

As Misty ran a brush through her wet hair, she put the call on speakerphone and told him about her morning, starting with the note and rose left on her porch.

"That's crazy, Misty," Brice said, and she could picture him running his fingers through his thick, blonde hair. "Who would have come by your house so early and left something like that on your porch?"

"I have no idea," she replied. "Harris just picked it up, but I doubt they'll find any fingerprints. Oh, did Dylan tell y'all about Pops' truck?"

"Yes, he called about an hour ago," he replied. "He said *you* found it? Misty, why were you out there by yourself?"

"Hey, I'm used to doing things on my own, remember?" she asked with a smile. "Look, as soon as I finish drying my hair, I'm going to Tori's neighborhood to talk to her neighbors. Maybe one of them has noticed something suspicious lately."

"I'll meet you there," Brice said.

When they pulled up in front of Tori's house

twenty minutes later, Misty spotted Mrs. Peterson across the road, watering her roses. She was in her late seventies and had lived in the same house for nearly fifty years. Misty and Brice knew she kept her eye on things and immediately went over to talk with her.

"Hi, Mrs. Peterson," Misty greeted the older woman with a friendly smile.

"Hey, kids," she replied in a slow, Southern drawl as she turned off the hose. "Is there any word on Tori?"

Misty would never cease to be amazed at the rate news traveled in this town. "No, ma'am, but that's actually why we're here," she replied.

"Have you noticed anything peculiar lately, Mrs. Peterson?" Brice asked. "Like someone hanging around Tori's house acting suspicious?"

Tapping her chin, Mrs. Peterson thought about it for a moment. "No, I don't think so," she replied. Just then, her eyes lit up and she snapped her fingers. "Wait, I just remembered something. A few nights ago, I was sitting on my front porch when I thought I heard someone humming. It sounded like it was coming from across the street, and in a little while, I saw a shadow running from around the back of Tori's house."

Her eyes widening, Misty asked, "What night was this, Mrs. Peterson?"

"It was Friday night," she replied. With a twinkle coming into her eyes, she smiled coyly at Brice and added, "I remember it particularly well, because shortly afterward, that good-looking grandfather of yours showed up and spent the night."

Both Misty and Brice's mouths dropped open in shock. Seeing the expressions on their faces, Mrs. Peterson blushed profusely and quickly added, "He spent the night with *Tori,* for goodness' sake, not with me!"

Blinking, Misty had to bite her lip to keep the laughter at bay. "Of course, Mrs. Peterson," she said.

Clearing his throat, Brice asked, "You didn't happen to see this shadow's face, did you?"

Still blushing, Mrs. Peterson shook her head and said, "No. He was dressed all in black with a hood covering his face."

"Thank you for your help, Mrs. Peterson," Misty said, reaching out to touch the older woman's arm. "If we have any more questions, we'll be in touch."

As they crossed the road, Misty muttered under her breath, "Now I see how rumors get started."

Chuckling, Brice said, "I know what you mean. And I'll bet Pops doesn't have a clue about Mrs. Peterson's little crush."

Just then, a loud creak caught Misty's attention, and she looked up to see Tori's new neighbor standing on his porch, watching them. Hayden Brownley was in his early to mid-forties, with thinning brown hair and mud-brown eyes. Misty had never officially met the man, but Tori had spoken of him a couple of times and Misty had seen him around town.

"Good afternoon," Misty greeted him.

"Hello," he replied with a small nod. "You're Tori's cousins, right?"

"I am," Brice said as they walked toward him. "I'm Brice, and this is Misty Raven, Tori's best friend."

"I've seen you over at Tori's house a few times since I moved in," Hayden said to Misty as he leaned across the porch railing and shook her hand. "It sure is a shame what happened to her."

"You haven't noticed anything unusual lately, have you?" Misty asked him.

Hayden's eyes narrowed slightly. "Like what?"

"Someone hanging around, acting strange," Misty replied. Pointing across the street, she added, "Mrs. Peterson said she saw someone a few nights ago dressed all in black and creeping around Tori's house. I thought perhaps you might have seen him, too?"

"I usually mind my own business and keep to myself," he replied rather stiffly. "If anything comes to mind, though, I'll be sure to let the police know."

As she and Brice returned to their cars, Misty stated drolly, "He certainly was a lot of help."

"Yeah, and his comment about minding his own business isn't at all like how Tori described him," Brice replied under his breath. "She said he was constantly asking nosy questions about her life while avoiding questions of his own."

"That's how most nosy people are," Misty

replied. "They want to know everything about everyone else, but don't want anyone asking questions about them."

"Kind of like you when you first arrived," Brice stated teasingly with a wink.

Misty couldn't help but laugh. "You got me there." Glancing at her watch, she said, "After we talk to a few more neighbors, do you want to get something to eat at *Pat's Kitchen*? It's Tuesday Tacos and Trivia tonight, and a lot of the townspeople will be there. Plus, I'm starving."

Brice agreed, and the two headed off down the street in the hope of finding someone who could give them some answers. Most of Tori's neighbors were at work, but the few that were home hadn't seen a thing. Misty tried not to feel discouraged, but the sound of a ticking clock kept pounding away inside her brain, telling her they were running out of time.

CHAPTER 6

Misty

It was after six o'clock when Misty and Brice walked into *Pat's Kitchen*. The restaurant was already filled with people, and the owner, Patrick Donovan, was standing just inside. When he spotted Misty and Brice, he immediately hurried over to join them.

"Is there any word on Tori?" he asked, his face filled with worry. He'd known Tori her whole life and had even taught her in middle school.

Brice shook his head. "Not yet," he replied. "Did you see her the day she disappeared?"

Mr. Donovan nodded. "Yes, I stopped by around ten o'clock that morning to ask about Neil and to get a cup of that wonderful coffee of hers."

"Was anyone else there?" Misty asked.

Mr. Donovan thought it over for a moment. "Jeremy Neely was there, of course. He goes in every Monday morning to do some writing. Oh, and I believe Noah Welch was there, too."

Jeremy Neely was a local author; Misty had first met him when she moved to Shady Pines last year. She didn't know Noah Welch, though, and looked at Brice questioningly.

"Noah went to school with us," Brice answered

the unasked question. Looking back at Patrick, he said, "Thank you, Mr. Donovan."

Nodding, Mr. Donovan led them to a corner booth, giving them a full view of the room. Misty spotted several familiar faces and planned to talk to as many of them as possible before the night ended.

After ordering their drinks, Misty absently twirled a strand of hair around her finger and stated thoughtfully, "I wonder if this would have happened if Tori had been able to go to Dahlonega with me."

Brice raised his eyebrows uncertainly. "I don't know, Misty. We may never know."

"She was so excited to go and help me find my father," Misty said, her heart tugging in her chest.

Brice leaned his elbows over on the table and said, "She's also the one who convinced you to try out that DNA website. Did you ever hear back from them?"

Misty sat back against the booth and sighed. "Yes. They found a match."

Brice blinked in surprise, and then his mouth dropped open. "Misty, that's wonderful!" he exclaimed after the shock had worn off. "Who is he? Have you contacted him yet? Why haven't you told me about this?"

Misty held up her hand and laughed. "Whoa, slow down. I don't know who he is because I haven't opened the email yet, which is why I haven't told you."

"Why on earth haven't you opened the email?" Brice wanted to know.

"I will," Misty assured him. "As soon as we find Tori. I just can't think about my father right now; not until we've found her."

Brice nodded understandingly. "Well, as soon as she's home, she's going to be thrilled to hear about this."

The server brought their tacos then, and as he slathered his food in salsa, Brice glanced at Misty uncertainly. After a moment, he set the salsa aside and said, "Look, Misty, I've been meaning to talk to you about Dahlonega, and…"

Before he could continue, a shadow fell across the table, and the two looked up to see Penny Atkins and her boyfriend, Theo.

"I've been so upset since I heard about Tori," Penny said, her perfectly red, manicured nails clutching Theo's arm. "Is there anything I can do before I leave?"

Misty had met Penny on multiple occasions and saw her often at church on Sundays. Penny and Tori had grown up together and shared several classes in high school, but the two were never close friends. Although Penny was nice enough, Misty had the feeling she thought she was better than everyone else. Her boyfriend, Theo, was from Savannah. He'd come to church with Penny several times, but no one knew how they'd actually met.

"Where are you going?" Brice asked Penny.

"I'm going to be in my cousin's wedding next

month, and she's taking her bridesmaids on a week-long trip to New York," Penny said with an excited smile. Turning to bat her eyes at her boyfriend, who had yet to say a word, she added, "Theo offered to house-sit while I'm away. Wasn't that thoughtful of him?"

Misty and Brice nodded. "Yes, very thoughtful," Misty replied. "I hope you enjoy your trip, Penny."

"Thanks," she said. "I hope that when I return, Tori will be back safe and sound."

As the two walked to their table, Misty asked, "Do you know anything about Theo?"

Brice shook his head. "Not really. Why?"

"Just curious." Misty shrugged. "He doesn't say much, does he?"

"I get the feeling he's after Penny's money," Brice stated.

Glancing at him curiously, Misty asked, "Is she rich?"

"She's an influencer and has around a million followers on social media," Brice replied. "She goes to Savannah all the time to take photos and rate restaurants and stuff."

"How did I not know this?" Misty questioned. "I guess I'm out of the loop when it comes to that kind of thing. I heard she and Theo connected through a dating app, but they must have met during one of her photoshoots in Savannah."

The two became quiet then as they enjoyed their tacos, and Misty couldn't help wondering what Brice had been about to say before Penny interrupted him. After their kiss on Devil's Cliff, Misty knew they'd need to talk about it eventually, but she was nervous to hear what Brice would say. She was a little grateful for Penny's interruption, as she didn't feel up to having a serious, heart to heart conversation right now.

When it was time for the trivia games to begin, some chose to stay at their own tables, while others gathered at larger tables. Misty and Brice joined the town's local veterinarian, Kyra Kirby, and her new boyfriend, Samuel Larson. When Brice spotted Noah Welch, he waved him over to their table.

"Have you met Misty?" Brice asked as soon as Noah sat down.

"Yes, I have," Noah replied, looking at Misty. "How are you, Miss Raven?"

Blinking in surprise, Misty stammered, "I'm, uh, doing okay. How are you?"

With a slight tightening of his jaw, Noah asked, "You don't remember meeting me, do you?"

Misty's cheeks flushed with embarrassment as she shook her head and said, "I'm sorry, but I'm afraid I don't."

Noah was one of those average height and weight kind of men, with curly red hair, a large nose, and dark blue eyes. Misty rarely forgot a face, and she wracked her brain, trying to remember when and where they'd met.

"We bumped into each other a few months ago at the market," he replied. Forcing a small smile, he shrugged and said, "Don't worry about it, though, Miss Raven. I'm easy to forget."

"Oh, I remember you now!" Misty exclaimed, snapping her fingers. "I accidentally bumped your buggy with mine and knocked your box of Cheerios onto the floor. You're the insurance agent, right?"

"Who stays cooped up in his house way too much," Brice added with a laugh, and Misty was grateful for the input. The air between her and Noah was feeling a little awkward, and she felt terrible for not immediately remembering him.

"I'm glad you've decided to start coming to trivia night, Noah," Brice added. "It'll be good for you."

"I guess," Noah muttered. With a sigh, he added, "I should really be at home, though, trying to fix my kitchen sink. It seems to be stopped up or something, and a plumber can't come out until Thursday. Can you imagine? It seems like everything just happens to me."

He continued to ramble about all of his woes, and once he finally finished, there was yet another awkward silence. After a moment, Brice cleared his throat and asked, "Isn't it awful about Tori? We're so worried about her."

Noah glanced down at his hands and nodded, but didn't say anything.

"Did you see her at all the day she disappeared?" Misty asked.

Noah glanced up at her. "Uh, I don't know..." he hesitated.

"Mr. Donovan said you were at her shop that day," Brice said.

Blinking, Noah fumbled around for a moment and then snapped his fingers, as if just remembering. "Oh, yes, I did stop by her shop. Everything seemed fine to me, though."

Before Misty could ask him anything further, Penny and Theo joined their group. Theo took the seat next to Misty, while Penny sat on his other side.

"So, you're from Savannah?" Misty asked Theo with a friendly smile.

Theo turned his piercing black eyes on Misty and just looked at her for a moment, not immediately responding. Finally, he nodded and said, "Yes, I am."

"I was doing a photoshoot downtown when it started to rain," Penny spoke up as she leaned around her boyfriend to look at Misty. "I was about to get completely soaked when Theo showed up out of nowhere with an umbrella. I call him my knight in shining armor."

"That's how you two met?" Misty asked as Penny beamed up at Theo, batting her long, fake eyelashes.

"Yes, isn't that *so* romantic?" Penny gushed.

Just then, Mr. Donovan stepped up to the mic to begin the trivia games, and their conversation ended. The questions were fun, and it was exciting to play on a team, but Misty noticed that Noah didn't participate very much. Theo, on the other hand, immediately came out of his shell and became very loud and competitive. Misty found his entire personality to be very complex, but his energy was helping their team to win, so she didn't mind at the moment. When he started insulting the other teams, however, Misty began to feel a little embarrassed. Penny, on the other hand, giggled and playfully slapped his arm.

They were up to the final question, and the excitement in the air was palpable as Mr. Donovan opened the last question.

"And the last question of the night is..." Mr. Donovan's voice trailed off as his eyes scanned over the paper and a look of confusion passed over his face. Silence filled the room as everyone waited to hear the question, but Mr. Donovan simply stood there, staring at the paper.

"Is he okay?" Misty heard Kyra mutter, and Misty looked over at Brice, noting his concerned expression.

"I-I don't understand," Mr. Donovan said in a shaky voice.

Brice and a few other men in the room stood up and hurried to his side, asking what was wrong. Misty watched closely as Brice took the note, but she was unable to read his lips as he quietly read what was written. When he raised his eyes to stare back at her in shock, she immediately stood and hurried to his side.

"Brice, what is it?" she whispered, leaning around his shoulder to look at the typewritten note.

"One has been taken. Will there be more? The clock is ticking toward Monday's dark door."

CHAPTER 7

I don't understand how that note got put into the stack of trivia questions," Mr. Donovan told the police once they arrived. "I wrote them up last night and locked them in my office desk."

"Apparently, someone broke into your office at some point and traded out the last trivia question for that note," Dylan said. "Who knows where you keep the questions hidden?"

Mr. Donovan sighed. "I suppose all of my staff knows by now, and my office *is* next to the restrooms. Perhaps someone has seen me getting them out of my desk in the past."

The restaurant was now closed, and everyone had been asked to stick around for questioning. Misty and Brice were giving Harris their statement while Mr. Donovan spoke with Dylan and Sheriff Ward in his office. Since the office was just down the hall, Misty could hear everything they were saying.

"Did either of you notice anything suspicious?" Harris asked Misty and Brice.

They both shook their heads. "No, we didn't," Brice answered, his tone heavy. He and Misty were terribly upset about the note, and although they hadn't wanted to tell Tori's parents, they'd decided to call them anyway. As horrible as it was, Amy and Neil deserved to know what was going on.

While Brice talked with Harris about the shoe prints found in the woods, Misty noticed Sheriff Ward step from the office and motion for Dylan to join him. The two stood just down the hall with their heads together, and by the scowl on Sheriff Ward's face, it looked like he was giving Dylan an earful. Misty couldn't be entirely certain, but she thought she caught the words "incompetent" and "finding another job" coming from the sheriff's lips. Dylan stood silently, his jaw clenching as he listened, and Misty wished she could hear everything that was being said.

Turning back to Brice and Harris, Misty said nonchalantly, "Sheriff Ward doesn't look happy."

Glancing down the hall, Harris sighed and said in a low voice, "It looks like he's giving Officer Mitchell what for again."

Brice frowned. "Again? Why?"

Harris shrugged. "I think he's just upset that this case hasn't been solved yet, and he's blaming Officer Mitchell for it."

"I'm sure Dylan is doing the best he can," Misty said softly.

Misty and Brice were told they could leave shortly after, and as they headed back out through the restaurant, everyone was talking about the note.

"Why risk breaking into the restaurant to leave that note?" Kyra's boyfriend, Samuel, spoke out.

"What was the point?"

"Do you think he plans to kidnap others?" Kyra asked in a worried tone.

"Poor Tori," Penny stated with a sigh.

"Seems like he enjoys playing games," Theo said.

"What do you mean?" Penny asked, her eyes growing wide.

"Ever heard of the Zodiac killer?" Theo asked, glancing around to see who all was listening. "He would send cryptic messages to the newspapers in a cat-and-mouse type of method. He enjoyed being chased and thought no one could ever catch him."

"You think that's what this guy is doing?" Noah wanted to know, eyeing Theo with a look that Misty couldn't quite decipher.

Theo leaned back in his chair and shrugged. "Who knows?"

As Misty and Brice left the restaurant, Misty played everything over in her mind. It was one thing to send letters and messages to a newspaper or even the police, but why break into a restaurant to place a threatening note into a stack of trivia questions? This case just kept getting more and more strange, but the one thing that weighed the most heavily on her mind was the last sentence of that note:

"The clock is ticking toward Monday's dark door."

Tori

Her eyelids were heavy, like they had weights resting upon them, and she felt as if she were swimming in a thick, black ocean. Consciousness tugged at her brain, calling for her to awaken, but something else told her to stay asleep; that evil was nearby.

The drugs in Tori's system were finally beginning to wear off, and she slowly shook her head and took a long, deep breath. Her skin was icy cold, but something warm whispered across her cheek. Frowning, Tori forced her eyes open and blinked, trying to focus on her surroundings.

"There you are."

The voice was right beside her ear, and with a startled gasp, Tori jerked her head in that direction. There, only inches away, was the horrible, distorted face of a man...or was it even human? The skin was ghostly white and the lips bright red, but the eyes were what frightened Tori the most. Rimmed with thick black circles, they stared back at her like two empty, lifeless shadows.

With a shriek that bounced loudly off the bare walls, Tori tried to jerk away, but he was much too quick. Catching her wrist, his icy cold fingers clamped tightly around her skin, stopping her in her tracks.

"Don't try to run away. I've been waiting much too long for you to wake up."

There was something a little different about his voice this time; it sounded oddly urgent and a bit more raspy. Forcing herself to turn and look back at him, Tori realized the horrible face staring back at her was a Halloween mask. Was that why he sounded different? Was the mask distorting his voice? He was sitting on the floor only inches away from her, and although the room was too dark to see the color of his eyes, she felt them piercing into hers all the same.

"Wh-why did you drug me?" she whispered, her entire body trembling as she pulled her arm away from his grasp.

"It seemed you were getting a bit too rowdy," he replied with a chuckle. Reaching out, he ran his finger along her cheek and added, "If you promise to behave from now on, perhaps you won't have to be drugged again."

Jerking her head out of his reach, Tori looked away and said, "I'll try to do better."

He didn't say anything for a moment; he simply sat there, silently watching her. Tori pulled her knees under her chin and stared down at the floor, terrified at what he may be planning to do with her. Suddenly, both his hands snaked out and he grabbed her around the ankles, yanking them out from under her. She screamed and kicked at him, but he was much larger and stronger, and before she could get away, he slammed her back against the ground and straddled her.

"This would go much easier if you didn't fight me," he said with a laugh as he pinned her hands over her head.

Just then, amidst the chaos and panic that ran madly through her head, Tori remembered something Dylan Mitchell had taught her during their self-defense classes. Taking a deep breath, she thrust her hips upward, throwing him off balance and giving her the window of opportunity she'd been hoping for. Within seconds, she'd flipped him over and jumped to her feet. Her eyes flew madly about the room as her mind screamed at her to escape while she had the chance. Launching herself toward the door, Tori flung it open and ran out.

The hallway was long and narrow, with dozens of closed doors lining either side. Not knowing which direction to go, Tori ran toward the door at the very end of the hall, hoping it would lead her outside. She could hear him coming after her, and the feeling of panic that nipped at her heels threatened to overcome her. What if that door didn't lead outside? What then? He'd kill her; she knew it.

The pounding of his footsteps as he drew closer beat inside Tori's head like a drum. She couldn't get one coherent thought inside her brain; all she could do was run like a wild, frantic animal.

Finally, she reached the door, and with trembling fingers, she twisted the knob and threw it open. On the other side was what appeared to be an exit staircase, and with adrenaline rushing through her veins, Tori raced across the threshold toward the stairs. Just before she reached the top step, a hand grabbed at her sleeve, throwing her off balance. With her eyes flying wide and mouth opening into a muted scream, Tori tumbled down the first flight of stairs, her body flailing about like a rag doll.

Moaning in pain, she lay in a heap at the bottom of the steps and watched as he slowly walked down toward her. Her body ached and her ankle felt like it might be broken, but none of it was as terrifying as what she feared he would do to her now.

"You shouldn't have done that," he said as he came to stand over her.

Tori tried to jerk away when he reached down and grabbed her by the arm, and she winced as his fingers tightened painfully around her already bruising skin. Without saying another word, he yanked her to her feet and dragged her back to her dark, cold prison cell.

When he pushed her back inside, not bothering to catch her when she fell to the ground, he said in a scathing tone, "Once I get through with your best friend, Misty Raven, you'll wish you hadn't just done that."

The slamming of the deadbolt blended with the sound of Tori's screams as she pushed herself to her feet to pound at the door, her shouts for him to leave Misty alone falling on deaf ears.

CHAPTER 8

Misty

The next morning, Misty slipped into her work clothes and went upstairs. She could always process her thoughts easier when working, and intended to lay everything out in her mind as she caulked the upstairs hallway.

She had just let Wally outside and was making herself a cup of coffee when she suddenly heard him begin to bark. He would often bark at squirrels or raccoons, but there was something different this time. There was a sound of ferociousness in his bark, and Misty quickly placed her coffee cup on the counter. Hurrying toward the door, she was reaching out to grab the doorknob when Wally's barking turned into a loud yelp of pain. Her heart nearly stopping, Misty yanked open the door to find her dog lying motionless out in the back yard.

Misty felt the blood drain from her face as she ran toward her pet, her mind whirling as she tried to process what could have happened. She didn't see any other animal or hear any sound other than the pounding of her own heart. Could he have had a seizure or heart attack? Was he even still alive?

With tears of panic filling her eyes, Misty dropped to her knees at Wally's side and reached out to touch his soft fur. "Wally? Sweetie, what's wrong?" she asked gently as she ran her hands over his massive body. He was still breathing, but his breaths were very shallow and he was drooling badly.

Suddenly, her fingers found a small, hard object buried close to the skin. When she separated his fur to take a closer look, she gasped in shock when she realized the object was a tranquilizer.

Just then, Misty felt the dark, heavy presence of someone stepping up behind her, but before she could react, a bag was thrown over her head and she was yanked roughly to her feet. Screaming, Misty tried to fight, but the man was too strong for her. With a firm, painful grip on her forearms, he dragged her across the yard and shoved her against what felt like the side of a car. With panic shooting through her veins, she bucked and kicked like a wild horse as he quickly zip-tied her wrists behind her back. The bag flew off her head, but before she could twist around to face her assailant, she was pushed into the car's trunk and the lid was slammed shut.

As the car bumped slowly down her driveway, Misty tried her best to free her wrists from the zip-tie. He may have managed to kidnap her, but she was going to be ready to fight as soon as he stopped and opened that trunk.

When the car turned from her driveway and out onto the main road, it began to go much faster, and the kidnapper started driving erratically. Misty was flung from one side of the trunk to the other, and she winced in pain when her head struck something solid. Fighting back the stars that floated before her eyes, she continued to try to get her hands out of the zip-tie, but the hard piece of plastic was fastened much too tightly.

As she continued to struggle, thought after thought flew madly through her mind. Was this the same man who had kidnapped Tori? What did he plan to do to her? Would he also kidnap others?

"One has been taken. Will there be more? The clock is ticking toward Monday's dark door."

The note left at Mr. Donovan's restaurant kept playing itself over and over in her mind, and Misty had to fight to keep herself from giving in to the panic that threatened to overcome her. Whether or not she could free herself of these binds, she planned to fight this man with every ounce of strength she had within her.

Just then, the car made a sudden turn, and within seconds, it skidded to a stop. Misty lay there, her heart pounding, as she waited for the trunk to open. Would she recognize him? Was he a member of their town, or would she come face to face with the infamous Julian Cooper? She tried to control the trembling of her body as she positioned herself in a way that she could kick him as soon as he opened the trunk. What she would do after that, she had no idea, but she had to at least try to escape.

Suddenly, the slamming of another car door met

her ears, and Misty's eyes widened when she heard what sounded like a struggle. Grunts and groans were muffled from where Misty lay, but when a body was slammed fiercely against the car, she jerked and pushed herself as far inside the trunk as she could. No words were spoken and no shouting could be heard; just deadly silence followed. Then, the crunching of footsteps and the slamming of two car doors filled the air. Listening intently, Misty heard the sound of a retreating vehicle, and then nothing.

What was happening? Who had her kidnapper been struggling with? Before she could ponder it any further, the trunk suddenly popped open, and Misty jerked back in fear, waiting for her attacker to reach in after her.

Sunlight poured into the dark abyss in which Misty lay, but no figure of a man stepped forward to block the beams. No hands reached in for her, and no voice called out with commands to climb from the trunk. Only silence met her ears, and as Misty slowly peered from the trunk, she realized her attacker had been taken away by the second car and the trunk had been opened with a key fob as the car left.

Misty managed to climb from the trunk without the use of her hands, and she stood there for a moment, looking around. She seemed to be in a desolate, lightly wooded area near the train tracks, but she could see the main road through the trees just up ahead. After memorizing the license plate number on the car, she hurried toward the road, hoping someone would drive by and help her. She tried to figure out exactly what had happened. Who was the second person? And why was she taken from her home, thrown into a trunk, and driven several miles outside of town just to be left behind? None of it made sense, but the sooner Misty could find help before he decided to come back, the better.

After walking over a mile down the lonely, desolate road that led to town, Misty finally saw a car approaching. She breathed a sigh of relief and began jumping up and down, hoping they wouldn't think she was crazy and keep driving. When the car slowed and swerved her way, a thought suddenly struck her and her heart caught. What if this was the kidnapper returning to take her back?

"Misty? Is that you?"

Squinting in the mid-morning sun, Misty saw Penny's boyfriend, Theo, emerging from the driver's side of the car with a look of confusion on his face.

"Oh, thank goodness," she breathed. Turning to show him the zip-tie around her wrist, she said, "Please help me, Theo. I was taken from my home and dumped at the railroad tracks."

Theo cut the tie from her wrists as Misty explained what had happened. When she climbed into his car a moment later, she felt utterly exhausted. As Theo turned his car around and headed back to town, he looked over at her with an expression of…concern? Disbelief? Or perhaps something else, but Misty was too tired and shaken to try to figure it out.

"Will you take me to my house?" Misty asked.

Raising his eyebrows, Theo said, "Sure, but I figured you'd want to go to the police first."

Using two fingers to massage her temple, Misty said, "Normally, I would, but my dog was shot with a tranquilizer, and I need to make certain he's alright."

Theo nodded, not saying another word. Misty glanced over at him, noting the piercing way his black eyes stared straight ahead, and she said, "Thank you, Theo. I don't know if I could have kept going if you hadn't come along."

Theo nodded. "You're welcome. I dropped Penny at the airport early this morning and was on my way to her house."

"Taking off work and staying at her house must be sort of like a vacation for you, too, huh?" Misty questioned, unable to stop herself from asking about his work. She wanted to know more about Penny's secretive boyfriend but was uncertain how much he was willing to share.

"Yes, I suppose so," was his short reply.

Sniffing, Misty decided to just be bold and ask point-blank. "Where *do* you work? If you don't mind my asking."

Theo turned down her driveway, and as shadows from the thick row of pine trees played along his face, he looked at her with one raised eyebrow and asked, "And what if I do mind?"

Misty blinked in surprise. "Oh, well, I didn't mean to..."

With a slightly mocking smile pulling at Theo's lips, he interrupted her and said, "I'm an artist."

"That's very interesting," she replied. When he didn't offer any further information, she asked, "Do you work for a particular company?"

Misty couldn't tell for certain, but it looked like Theo's jaw tightened in irritation. In a clipped tone, he stated, "I work for a sign-making shop near Victory Drive."

Before she could ask the name of the shop, Theo parked in front of her house, and Misty was immediately sidetracked with concern for Wally. With her heart in her throat, she jumped from the car and ran around the side of her house, half expecting to find Wally lying there, dead. What she did find, however, was nothing. She stood there for a moment in surprise and slowly looked around. Wally was nowhere to be found.

CHAPTER 9

Fighting panic, Misty ran into her house in search of her phone. She intended to call Brice or Adam or someone to come help her search for Wally, but as soon as she unlocked the screen, she saw several missed calls from Patrick Donovan and a voice message.

"Misty, this is Patrick Donovan," he said on her voicemail. *"Are you alright? I just stopped by your house this morning to, uh, talk to you about something, when I found Wally lying out in the backyard. I can't get you to answer the door or your phone, so I'm taking him to the vet. I hope that's okay. Please call me back as soon as you get this."*

Feeling relieved, Misty grabbed her purse and ran back outside. Theo was still waiting, so she told him what had happened.

"I'm going by the vet first, and then I'll go see Officer Mitchell at the police station," she explained. "Thank you again, Theo, for rescuing me."

Nodding, Theo didn't say a word; he simply climbed back into his car and drove away. As Misty drove out behind him, she suddenly wondered how he'd known where she lived; she never gave him her address when she'd asked him to drive her home. When Theo turned his car in the direction of Penny's house, Misty couldn't help but wonder if Penny knew him well enough to allow him full access to her house and all of her belongings.

When Misty arrived at the vet moments later, she rushed inside to find Patrick Donovan sitting in the waiting room alone. He wore a pinched, worried expression, and when he spotted Misty, he immediately stood to his feet.

"Misty, thank goodness," he said with a sigh. "I had just decided to give you ten more minutes to get in touch before I was calling the police."

"How is Wally? Is he going to be okay?" Misty wanted to know.

Patrick nodded toward the back room. "I don't know yet; Kyra and her assistant, Anna, are with him now." Looking back at Misty, he asked, "What exactly happened?"

Taking a seat in one of the nearby chairs, Misty told him everything. By the time she'd finished, Mr. Donovan was so upset, he was pacing back and forth around the room.

"Misty, this is terrible," he said, running his fingers through his salt-and-pepper hair. "And it doesn't make any sense. Someone apparently intervened, but why leave you there?"

Misty shook her head. "I don't know. Perhaps he took the kidnapper away, but before he could come back for me, something happened."

Just then, the door to the back room opened, and Kyra Kirby stepped out. Her flaming red hair was piled high on top of her head, and she wore bright green glasses to match her green eyes. Stepping out beside her was Kyra's young assistant, Anna Douglas.

"Is Wally okay?" Misty immediately asked as she stood quickly to her feet.

Kyra nodded. "Yes, sweetie, he's going to be just fine. The tranquilizer drug was a bit too strong and probably would have killed him if Patrick hadn't come along when he did. I've administered a reversal drug, so he should wake up within the next thirty minutes or so. If you'd like to leave him here until four o'clock, I will keep an eye on him and make certain he's acting normal."

Misty breathed a long sigh of relief at the good news; she'd been so afraid that he would die. With a nod, she agreed to come back later and pick Wally up.

"I know how relieved you are, Misty," Anna said in her typical soft voice as she stepped closer to Misty and gently touched her arm. "I don't know what I'd do without my Cocker Spaniel."

Smiling at Kyra's new pretty, blonde-haired assistant, Misty squeezed her hand and said, "Our pets are special to us, aren't they?"

Anna nodded. "They sure are." Hesitating, she bit her lower lip for a moment and then finally asked, "Has...has there been any word on Tori? I've been praying for her."

Misty sighed and shook her head. "Not that I know of."

Misty had first met Anna at church a few months

ago and learned that the shy young woman was a few years younger than her. Anna was going to college to become a veterinarian, so Kyra had recently hired her as an assistant. So far, Anna seemed to be doing a great job.

"I hope they find her soon," Anna said, her soft blue eyes filling with tears.

Kyra asked Anna to check on one of the cats then, and Misty promised she'd let Anna know as soon as she heard anything about Tori.

After paying Kyra and thanking her for helping Wally, Misty walked out to her car with Mr. Donovan at her side.

"Thank you *so* much, Mr. Donovan," she said, reaching out to squeeze his arm. "If not for you, Wally might have died."

Patting her hand, Mr. Donovan said, "You're quite welcome. I'm just glad I could help."

He seemed to have something else he wished to say, but when Misty announced she'd better get to the police station, he nodded and asked her to keep him updated.

As Misty told him goodbye and drove away, she thought of how blessed she was to have found Shady Pines. She'd really never been part of a community before, and knowing that she now lived in a town filled with friends who cared about her meant the world.

When she arrived at the police station, she walked back to Dylan's office and poked her head inside. He was sitting behind his desk with his cell phone pressed against his ear, and when he saw her, he motioned for her to come in.

While she waited for the phone call to end, Misty walked slowly around the room, taking in the few personal items Dylan had sitting around. His license and certification hung in picture frames on the wall, and Misty noticed his dog tags hanging from a nail on the bookshelf. The bookshelf itself had several research-type books filling its space, along with a few fictional detective novels. As Misty continued around the room, she spotted a group picture with several men dressed in military uniforms. Dylan was standing front and center, his face stern and his stance rigid. Misty knew he hadn't been out of the military for very long and wondered why he'd left.

"What can I do for you, Misty?"

She'd been so engrossed in her own thoughts that Misty hadn't realized Dylan was off the phone. Taking a deep breath, she sat in the chair across from his desk and told him the whole story. Once she was finished, she jumped in surprise when a gruff voice spoke out from behind.

"How exactly has our town gone from a safe haven to a place where kidnappers are snatching women off the streets left and right?"

Turning, Misty saw that Sheriff Ward was standing in the doorway, his face as red as fire. He'd apparently heard what had happened and was glaring at Dylan like it was his fault.

"Sir, you know we're trying our best to find this

guy…" Dylan began but was quickly cut off when Sheriff Ward stepped further into the room and pointed his finger into the detective's face.

"Obviously, you're not trying hard enough, Mitchell," he snapped. "Where is the ballistics report I asked for yesterday on that shoe print we found behind Barlow's Hardware?"

Dylan's brow furrowed in confusion. "I put it on your desk last night."

Sheriff Ward shook his head. "No, you didn't. I spoke with Sam at the front desk, and he said you took it home with you. That's not allowed, Mitchell, and you know it."

His jaw clenching, Dylan stood to his feet and said in a steely tone, "I did *not* take it home, and I don't appreciate being accused of doing so."

The two men sized each other up for a moment, and the silence between them sizzled. With a small cough to remind the men she was still there, Misty asked softly, "Do you need anything else from me, or should I just go home?"

Tearing his gaze away from Dylan, Sheriff Ward looked at Misty and his expression softened. "I'm sorry, Miss Raven," he said. "You needn't have witnessed that. I'm just so upset that this is happening…" he paused and cleared his throat. "Well, anyway. Are you alright? Did this man hurt you in any way?"

Misty shook her head. "No, not really. I believe he would have, though, if the second person hadn't shown up."

Rubbing the stubble on his chin, Sheriff Ward muttered, "It's all very strange." He then looked at Dylan and said in a stern tone, "Get her full statement and have the report, along with the one I requested yesterday, on my desk within the hour."

After the sheriff stomped out, Dylan looked at Misty apologetically and said, "Sorry about that. We're all a little on edge right now."

Misty responded with a small half-smile. "I understand," she said. Chewing on her bottom lip thoughtfully, she asked, "Did you really not take that report home?"

Dylan shook his head. "No, and I intend to find out why Sam said I did," he stated. Grabbing his pen and notepad, he said, "Let's go over everything once more, so I'm sure I have it all written down correctly."

Misty repeated the story, her eyes widening when she realized she'd missed a part. "Oh, I almost forgot," she said, leaning forward with excitement. "I memorized the tag number of the car I was in."

"Smart thinking, Misty," Dylan said. As he jotted down the number, Misty suddenly noticed a bandage wrapped around his wrist.

"How did you hurt your wrist?" she asked him.

Glancing down at his hand, Dylan pulled the cuff of his sleeve over the bandage and said, "Oh, I cut it on a wire last night."

Silence filled the air as Dylan finished writing

his notes, and Misty wondered what kind of wire he'd been cut with. She studied him for a moment, suddenly realizing how little she knew about him.

"Where are you from, Dylan?" she asked, breaking the silence.

Dylan looked up at her in surprise. "I'm from the Jacksonville area," he replied. "Why do you ask?"

Misty shrugged. "It just hit me that we've known each other for almost a year now and you know so much about me, but I know so little about you. What brought you to Shady Pines?"

"When I was in the army," he said, absently twirling his pen between his fingers, "I was stationed in Savannah for a little while. Although I love Savannah, it's too big for my taste. So, after doing a bit of traveling around outside the city, I thought Shady Pines was the best place for me to settle down."

"Why not go back to Jacksonville?" she wanted to know.

"I haven't lived there for over fifteen years," he stated matter-of-factly. "Why go back now?"

"Don't you have family there?" she asked.

"No."

His response was short and clipped, and Misty had the feeling he didn't wish to continue with the conversation. Was he just the overly personal type, or was there something in his past that he wished to hide?

Clearing his throat, Dylan held up the notes he'd written down and said, "Anyway, I'll look into all of this and let you know what we find out. Hopefully, we're going to catch this guy soon."

Misty nodded and stood. "Thanks, Dylan."

As Misty left the station, she casually glanced toward the front desk and stopped in surprise. Kyra Kirby's new boyfriend, Samuel, was working there, and it dawned on Misty that he must be the "Sam" Sheriff Ward was referring to. She hadn't realized he worked at the station, and when he spotted her standing there staring at him, he threw up his hand in a friendly wave.

"Hi, Miss Raven," he greeted her with a smile.

She was about to go over and ask him about the missing ballistics report when a man carrying a helmet and wearing a leather biker's vest stalked inside and slammed a speeding ticket down on the desk in front of Samuel. The man was apparently very angry, and not wishing to witness a confrontation, Misty waved back to Samuel and quickly hurried outside.

As Misty drove toward her house, she couldn't help wondering why Sheriff Ward was riding Dylan so hard. She knew Dylan was doing his best to solve this case and find Tori, but it almost seemed as if the sheriff had developed a chip on his shoulder toward the young detective.

Spotting a sign on the road that mentioned Savannah, Misty made a last-minute decision and turned her car in that direction. It had been a while since she'd last visited the beautiful city, and she wanted to check into Theo's story about working at a sign shop. She wasn't sure why, but there was something about him that made her think he might have something to hide.

CHAPTER 10

Thirty minutes later, Misty pulled into the parking lot of *Master's Sign Shop.* She wasn't sure this was the right place, but after searching online for sign-making shops near Victory Drive, this was the only one that showed up. As she walked inside, she wished she'd thought to ask Theo his last name. If he would have told her, that is.

"Hello there," a man in his early forties greeted her when she entered. "How can I help you?"

"Hello," Misty responded with a smile. "I'm looking for Theo. Is he here?"

With a look of surprise, the man shook his head and asked, "Theo Dodge? No, ma'am, he hasn't worked here in over two months."

Raising her eyebrows, Misty asked, "Really? He told me recently that he worked here."

Huffing, the man replied, "Theo tells people a lot of things. Is there anything I can help you with? I'm the manager."

"I'm planning to open a bed-and-breakfast in the next few months, so I'll be needing a nice wooden sign," Misty replied. "Can you give me some prices?"

Nodding his head eagerly, the man pulled out a pricing list and offered Misty a chair. He went over their prices first and then showed her some photos of wooden signs they'd done in the past. Misty was quite impressed, and after she told him exactly what she wanted, he said he'd email her an official quote.

As he jotted down her email, Misty casually asked, "So, why did Theo quit?"

The manager sighed and shook his head. "Because he doesn't really want to work anywhere," he replied with a bit of disgust in his voice. He then looked at her with wide eyes and asked, "Is he, uh, a good friend of yours?"

"No, not at all," Misty replied. "He's dating a friend of mine, though, so that's how I know him."

"You may need to tell your friend to run from him," he stated. "Theo is...well, let's just say he's different."

Before Misty could ask what he meant by that, another customer walked in and started asking questions, so Misty said goodbye and left. When she got into her car, she searched for Theo Dodge online and found an address. Curious to see where he lived, she drove to the mobile home park listed in the directions. What she hadn't been prepared for when she arrived, though, was how much disrepair the park was in. Trash lay scattered all over the ground, and Misty spotted what appeared to be a homeless camp in the woods just beside the park.

Pulling her car in front of one of the worst-looking trailers there, Misty got out and slowly walked around the small home. A couple of the windows were broken, and the outside frame was covered in mildew. Grass and weeds had grown knee high, and Misty shivered as a snake quickly slithered beneath the trailer. As bad as the exterior looked, Misty could only imagine what the inside must look like.

Had Theo ever brought Penny out here? If Penny really was as well off as Brice had said, Misty couldn't imagine her dating such a slob.

"Can I help you?"

Surprised, Misty turned to find a man in his early thirties standing only a few feet away. His hair was long and greasy, and his bare arms were covered in tattoos. He was staring at her with narrowed, suspicious eyes, and Misty immediately realized it had probably been a bad idea to come out here alone.

Clearing her throat, she forced a smile and said, "I was looking for Theo. Is he home?"

His eyes narrowing even further, the man stepped closer and asked, "No, he ain't. You know where he might be hiding?"

Misty blinked. "Uh, hiding?"

Spitting out a string of dark brown tobacco, he stated, "Yeah. He owes me nearly a thousand G's and I ain't seen him in almost three weeks."

"Well, if I see him, I'll let him know you're looking for him," Misty said. When the man's eyes dropped to her purse, she tightened her hold on its strap and asked, "What is your name?"

With a steely look on his face, the man moved closer until he stood only a few inches away. Misty could smell the alcohol on his breath, and it was all she could do to maintain a neutral expression.

"Just tell him that Blaze wants his money back," he snarled. "He'll know who you're talkin' about."

Swallowing past the lump in her throat, Misty nodded and slowly stepped around him. "I'll do that," she said and then made a mad dash for her car.

Jumping inside, she quickly locked the doors, cranked the engine, and drove away as fast as she could. Just before turning the corner, she glanced back and saw that "Blaze" had walked out into the road and was staring after her.

Twenty minutes later, Misty was stuck in traffic. Apparently, there had been an accident, and her phone said it would take nearly two hours to get home. With a moan, Misty regretted coming to Savannah so late in the day. Now, poor Wally would have to spend the night at the vet.

When her phone started to ring and she saw Patrick Donovan's name flash across her car's screen, her heart caught. Had something else happened?

"Misty, I hate to bother you," he said when she answered, "but when I stopped by your house this morning, I wanted to talk to you about something.

Could I possibly stop by again now?”

"I had to come to Savannah for, uh, something," she replied, "and I am currently stuck in traffic. It looks like I won't be home until after 5 o'clock."

"Oh, no," Patrick exclaimed. "What about Wally?"

"I guess I'll just have to get him in the morning," she said with a sigh.

"Why don't I pick him up for you?" Mr. Donovan offered.

"Oh, I couldn't ask you to do that…"

"You didn't ask," he stated. "I offered. The restaurant isn't busy at all today, so I can go get him now. Is that alright with you?"

Misty smiled with relief. "That would be perfect," she said. After letting him know where she kept the spare key to her house hidden, she said, "Thank you so much, Mr. Donovan. I really hated to leave Wally at the vet all night after what he's been through today."

After they'd hung up, Misty began to wonder what he needed to talk to her about. Was it something to do with the note he'd found on trivia night? Had something else happened that she hadn't heard about yet?

With a sigh, Misty turned on some relaxing music and tried to clear her mind. The traffic was barely moving, so it seemed like she really would be stuck here for a while.

"Anna, honey, I'm going over to check on Mrs. Johnson's cat," Kyra Kirby called from her office. "You know how forgetful Mrs. Johnson is, and I want to make sure she's keeping Simba's incision clean. I'll be back before closing time. Would you like me to bring you something to eat since you barely ate anything for lunch?"

Anna Douglas smiled to herself as she walked toward the kennels. Kyra, her boss, constantly told her she was too thin and tried to talk her into going out to eat with her nearly every day. What Kyra didn't know was that Anna could barely afford the groceries to make herself a ham sandwich every day, much less pay for a meal at *Pat's Kitchen* or the local pizzeria.

"No, thanks, Kyra," Anna called out. "I'll eat when I get home. While you're gone, I'm going to spend some time with Paisley; she's still a little groggy from her surgery."

As Anna opened the cage door to the sweet little Sheltie's kennel, she heard Kyra go out the back way and then the sound of her car engine revving to life.

"Hi, girl," Anna said softly as she sat on the hard floor next to the groggy dog.

Wagging her tail, Paisley moved her head from the blanket she was curled up on to rest her nose against Anna's leg.

"You're such a sweet thing," she said as she gently rubbed Paisley's ears. When the animals first awakened after surgery, they were always confused and could easily become upset. Anna tried to make a point to sit with them for a while once they began to awaken, as the company brought them comfort and helped them to stay relaxed.

As she sat there, softly humming, she got so lost in thoughts of school and this month's rent, and all the shelter dogs she was supposed to help with this weekend that she lost all track of time. When she heard the back door open, her eyes widened and she quickly got to her feet. Kyra was back already, and she hadn't finished with the files *or* cleaned out little Tiger's litter box yet.

"How is Simba's incision, Kyra?" she called out as she left the dog kennels and hurried down the hall toward the cat room.

When Kyra didn't answer, Anna thought maybe she was hearing things. She paused to listen for the jingling of Kyra's long earrings but was greeted instead by a sudden, loud bark from the kennel. Frowning, she hurried back down the hall to see what was wrong with Berkeley, the German Shepherd that was boarding with them this week. She opened the door and walked back into the room she'd just left, shielding her ears from the loud, ferocious-sounding barks. Berkeley was in a cage around the corner, and as Anna walked that way, the lights suddenly shut off. The barking stopped, and the room was filled with an eerie, deathly silence.

Just then, the slow ***clip-clop*** of shoes tapping against cement echoed throughout the room. Turning around, Anna searched the shadows for Kyra, wondering why her boss was being so quiet and acting so…so strange.

"Anna."

The deep, husky voice was amplified in the large, barren room, and it seemed to echo inside Anna's brain. Her heart catching, she spun around in the direction of the voice, but before her eyes could focus on the large shadow behind her, a gloved hand holding a towel quickly covered her face. Within just a few moments, Anna slipped into unconsciousness and slumped to the floor.

CHAPTER 11

Misty

When Misty pulled into her driveway at a little after five o'clock, she saw that Mr. Donovan's car was parked in front of her house. Hurrying inside to greet her beloved pet, she found Wally in the kitchen, happily licking up a bowl of what appeared to be chicken and rice.

"Kyra said to give him something bland to eat when I got him home," Mr. Donovan explained. "I wasn't sure when you'd be back, and he acted like he was starving."

Rubbing her dog's soft ears as he finished his meal, Misty said, "Thank you so much, Mr. Donovan, for taking care of him. I'm so relieved that he's going to be okay."

"You're quite welcome," he replied with a smile. "Would you like me to fix **you** something to eat? You've had a pretty rough day, and I imagine you're tired and hungry."

"Oh, I've put you out enough..." Misty stopped when Mr. Donovan held up his hand.

"Nonsense," he replied. "I'll whip you up some of the best pancakes you've ever tasted. If you don't mind eating breakfast for supper, that is?"

With a laugh, Misty said, "I actually love

breakfast for supper."

As Mr. Donovan cooked, Misty went into her bedroom to change into something more comfortable. She'd just finished pulling her hair into a high ponytail when her eyes landed on the stack of photographs lying on her dresser. They were of her mother, Elena. She'd gotten them from Merrick Levine last week during her visit to Dahlonega. Merrick owned Black Wolf Lodge and was an old friend of her mother's who'd once been deeply in love with her.

Picking up the top photo, Misty smiled at the look of happiness on her beautiful mother's face, and her heart squeezed in her chest. After all these years of searching and looking for answers, she'd finally found them, and with just one click, she would know who her real father was.

With a sigh, Misty returned the picture to the pile and hurried back into the kitchen, where a heavenly smell wafted through the air. Mr. Donovan had not only prepared pancakes but also scrambled eggs and bacon. Her mouth watering, Misty quickly fixed them both a cup of hot tea and sat down at the table.

"So, you never told me how your trip to Dahlonega went," Patrick said as they both began to eat the delicious meal.

Misty smiled. "It's funny you'd mention that, because I was just in my bedroom, looking at some photos of Mom that someone in Dahlonega gave me."

"Oh? Does that mean you found some answers?"

"Sort of," Misty replied as she poured a heaping amount of syrup over her stack of pancakes. "Mom worked at the lodge where we stayed, so I met several people who knew her. Merrick Levine, one of the owners, gave me the photos and one of Brice's friends gave me some letters that Elena wrote to his mother after she left Dahlonega."

"Did you find anything in the letters?" Mr. Donovan asked.

Misty nodded. "Yes. Apparently, my father's name was Ricky. Do you know of anyone in the area named Ricky? She wrote about seeing him here in Shady Pines when she and Karson first moved here."

When Patrick didn't immediately answer, Misty looked up at him questioningly. It was then she realized how pale he'd suddenly become.

"Mr. Donovan, are you alright?" she asked, reaching out to touch his hand.

Standing to his feet abruptly, Patrick walked to the kitchen counter, and with his back to her, he rested his hands on its hard surface. Misty could see his knuckles growing white from the way he gripped the counter, and she was immediately concerned that he'd become sick.

Before Misty could stand up and try to help him, he spun back around to face her. His cheeks were still pale, and when he cleared his throat to speak, Misty was not at all prepared for what he had to say.

"Misty, the reason I wanted to talk to you is because…because I think that *I'm* your father."

CHAPTER 12

Tori

A door slamming, footsteps, and then the sound of a woman crying echoed out in the hallway. Was she losing her mind? Tori pressed her ear against the cold, metal door of her room and listened. No, she wasn't losing her mind; those sounds were real.

Tears filled her eyes as a panicked hiccup caught in the back of her throat. Was it Misty she was hearing? He'd said her friend would pay for Tori's actions. Had he kidnapped her as well? What would they do to her?

The door to the room next to Tori's opened, and then a *thud* met her ears just before the door slammed shut and was locked. The crying grew louder, and Tori hurried as quickly as her swollen ankle would allow toward the wall that separated the two rooms.

Ramming her knuckles against the wall, Tori cried out, "Misty! Is that you?"

The crying stopped, and after a moment of hesitation, a trembling voice called out, "T-Tori?"

Tori blinked when she realized it wasn't Misty's voice she heard. Relief flooded over her, and then her heart squeezed when it struck her to whom the voice belonged.

Anna Douglas, the young vet assistant, was the kidnapper's second victim.

Misty

Misty stared open-mouthed at Mr. Donovan, feeling utterly and completely dumbfounded. Had he really just said he thought he was her father?

Shaking her head in an attempt to clear it, Misty asked hoarsely, "W-what did you just say?"

Mr. Donovan was so frazzled, he looked as if he either wanted to cry or bolt from the room. "I don't even know where to begin," he said, his face flushed. Pulling his phone from his pocket, he opened the screen and held it up for Misty to see. "A few years ago," he said, "my wife and I signed up for one of those DNA websites. We both wanted to know more about our families and such, but I'd completely forgotten about it until this morning when…when I was looking through my emails and realized I'd received a message from the website that said I had a match."

Misty read the email on Mr. Donovan's phone, one that looked exactly like the email she'd received. With a trembling finger, she tapped on the link. There, in black and white, it said that Patrick Donovan and Misty Raven shared fifty percent DNA, which could only mean one thing. They were father and daughter.

Misty slowly raised her eyes to stare up at…her father? How was this possible? Her mind was so fuzzy that she could barely get a clear thought.

"I'm, uh, a little confused," she said, laying the phone down to rub her eyes. "How can you possibly be my father?"

Mr. Donovan sat back in his chair, and Misty suddenly wondered why she hadn't noticed how bloodshot his eyes were until now. She'd simply thought he was upset about everything that had happened that morning, but apparently, there was more to it than that.

Taking a deep breath, Mr. Donovan slowly blew it out and opened his mouth to begin the story. Before he could utter one single word, however, Misty's cell phone rang. Glancing down, she saw Brice's name flashing across the screen, and thinking it could be about Tori, she answered it.

"Misty, can you talk?" he asked as soon as she answered.

Glancing over at her guest, Misty said, "Well, I'm sitting here talking with Mr. Donovan…"

"Put me on speakerphone then, will you?" he interrupted. "I want to tell both of you something."

Her forehead wrinkling, Misty put the call on speakerphone and said, "Alright, we're both listening. Is something wrong?"

"I just saw Harris in town," he began. "He told me that around 4:00 this afternoon, Anna Douglas was kidnapped."

Misty gasped, her eyes flying open wide with shock. "What? But Mr. Donovan just left the vet!"

"Yes, I left around 3:30," Mr. Donovan spoke up after glancing at his wristwatch. "Anna was perfectly alright when I left."

"Well, Dylan stopped by to talk to Kyra about the tranquilizer Wally was shot with and found the place in a mess," Brice explained. "The front door was half open, and when Dylan went inside, he discovered a note written across one of the back walls in spray paint."

"What did it say?" Misty wanted to know.

"*Two are now gone. How many more will I take? Monday is just around the corner, so keep in mind what's at stake,*" Brice replied. "Kyra had just gone to check on a patient and wasn't there when it happened. Look, Harris said he was heading to the vet to help go over the crime scene. I'm going to pick up Aunt Amy and Uncle Neil and the three of us are going to wait in the vet parking lot so we can know as soon as there are any updates."

Standing to her feet, Misty said, "I'll meet y'all there."

After hanging up the phone, Misty grabbed her purse and was heading out of the kitchen when she realized Patrick was still there. Turning to look at him, she cleared her throat awkwardly and said, "I'm, uh, sorry to rush off like this. In all honesty, though, I'd like to have some time to process all of this before you and I talk further."

A look of hurt flashed across Patrick's face, but

he quickly covered it with a tight smile and said, "I completely understand." Stuffing his hands into the pockets of his pants, he followed her outside without another word. When they reached the front porch, he looked at her with what appeared to be pain in his eyes and said softly, "I'm sorry, Misty. I-I know you don't wish to talk right now, but please know that I never realized I had a child. If I had..."

Not trusting her feelings at the moment, Misty stepped away from him and said in a clipped tone, "We'll talk later. Right now, I need to focus on finding my friend."

With that being said, Misty turned and walked to her car without looking back.

CHAPTER 13

When Misty arrived at the vet clinic, police cars and local citizens already filled the parking lot. As Misty made her way over to stand with the Barlow family, she listened to the worried whispers that drifted throughout the crowd. Everyone was concerned about the two missing women, and they were all wondering who would be next.

Brice and Mrs. Amy were standing beside Mr. Neil, who was seated in a wheelchair, and Misty was surprised to find that Pops was also with them.

"How are you both feeling?" she asked the two men.

"Worried," Mr. Neil replied in a heavy tone. It was obvious he was still on medication for his leg, and Misty knew he needed to be at home resting.

"Worried sick," Pops said. There were black circles lining his eyes, and he still wore a bandage on the back of his head. "Nothing like this has ever happened in our town before."

Misty patted him on the back. "Let's just hope the police can find something in there," she replied, nodding toward the clinic.

"Hey, Brice, what's going on? Has something happened?"

Misty turned to find that Noah Welch had approached Brice, and as the two talked, she spotted Adam Dawson and his sister, Lexi, standing not very far away. She hadn't realized Lexi was back in town, and when she went over to speak to her, she noticed a car driving slowly by. Squinting her eyes, she realized the driver was Theo. He stared out at the scene before him with an odd expression on his face, and when he spotted Misty watching him, he jerked his eyes back toward the road ahead and sped away. She wondered why he wasn't out at Penny's house, but then assumed he must have needed something at the market.

"Hi, Lexi," Misty greeted Adam's sister with a smile.

"Misty, it's so good to see you," Lexi gushed as she pulled Misty into a hug.

"Was Anna kidnapped?" Adam asked, his black eyes scanning over the clinic and police cars.

Misty nodded. "Yes, she was."

Lexi tucked a straight, silky strand of dark hair behind her ear and shivered. "How awful. If I'd known a kidnapper was on the loose, I'd have stayed in Atlanta instead of coming down to visit for a week."

Misty talked with Lexi and Adam for a moment longer, and as she headed back to join the Barlow family, she accidentally bumped into someone.

Glancing up, she realized the man was Hayden Brownley, Tori's neighbor.

"Oh, excuse me, Mr. Brownley," she apologized as she took a step back.

With a surprisingly friendly smile, he waved a hand in the air and said, "That's alright. And you can call me Hayden." Looking around, he asked, "What's happened here?"

"Anna Douglas was kidnapped a few hours ago," she replied. "Do you know her?"

Hayden shook his head. "No, I don't think so. Do they know if it's the same guy that took Tori?"

"I don't know," Misty replied with a shrug, "but I'm assuming so."

Hayden shook his head and made a *tsking* sound with his mouth. "The police had better do a better job of protecting the women around here," he stated.

Studying him as he spoke, Misty asked, "Was there much crime where you came from?"

Glancing at her with a bit of surprise in his mud-brown eyes, Hayden said, "No, there wasn't."

With an innocent smile, Misty asked, "I forget where you said that was?"

"I don't believe I ever did say," he replied with a sly grin. Nodding at her, he added, "Have a good evening, Miss Raven. And be careful," before he turned and sauntered away.

Pursing her lips in irritation, Misty continued on toward the Barlows.

"Poor Anna," Noah was saying to Brice when

Misty reached the two men.

"Do you know her very well?" Misty asked, politely butting in.

Noah nodded. "Sort of," he replied, and then added with a sigh, "She's been taking care of my cat, Tiger. I sure hope he's okay."

Before Misty could talk to him further, Harris came around from the back of the clinic and headed toward his patrol car. Grabbing the opportunity, Misty hurried over to ask about the investigation.

"Were y'all able to find anything?" she asked hopefully.

Harris took off his glasses and rubbed his tired eyes. "Not really," he replied in a heavy voice. Then, as if realizing he should have kept that bit of information to himself, he quickly added, "But the guys are still back there, going over everything. We're hopeful this guy left *something* we can trace."

"What about the shoe print y'all found behind Barlow's Hardware?" she asked, thinking of the report Sheriff Ward said he never received.

Harris replaced his glasses, and with a thoughtful look, he said, "I believe Officer Mitchell has that report, but Samuel said he heard from the lab guy that the shoe print was from one of those military types of hiking boots."

Misty blinked in surprise and asked, "Are you sure?"

Harris shrugged. "That's what he said. Look,

Miss Raven, Sheriff Ward will have my hide if he catches me sharing information with you. Please, don't tell him I've told you anything."

Misty nodded. "I won't, Harris."

As Misty rejoined the Barlow family, she noticed Noah talking pretty intently with Kyra Kirby's boyfriend, Samuel. She looked around for Kyra, but didn't see her, and assumed she must be too shaken up to be there. Why was Samuel here, though, and not manning the desk back at the station? She made a mental note at that moment to find out more about him.

Two hours later, Sheriff Ward appeared on Shady Pines' local news station. He stood in front of the clinic, and while half the town watched from the parking lot, he gave a statement regarding Anna's kidnapping.

"If anyone has **any** information regarding the whereabouts of Anna Douglas or Tori Barlow, please come forward." After a slight hesitation, Sheriff Ward added in a heavy tone, "I think it's best to also put the town on alert for the time being. There's a kidnapper on the loose, and until we can find him, everyone should be extremely careful. Please, stay in groups, don't go out alone late at night, and if you see anything suspicious, call us immediately."

After the cameras were cut off, Misty watched

as Sheriff Ward called Dylan to the side. With a clenched jaw, he hissed, "I didn't want it to get to this point, Mitchell. Putting the town on alert means I will now have to deal with the mayor breathing down my neck. Find this guy, Dylan. *Please.*"

"I'm doing my best, sir," Dylan replied, his face solemn.

The entire town was tense and on edge; Misty could feel the unease making its way through the crowd like a deadly vapor. Mothers were holding their children extra close, while a look of fear filled the eyes of every young woman around. What most people didn't know, however, was a third kidnapping attempt had already been made only that morning. What if that unknown man hadn't saved Misty? What if she was also hidden away somewhere at this very moment, frightened out of her mind and not knowing what was going to happen to her?

"We've got to find them, Brice," Misty whispered. "Before it's too late."

His jaw tense, Brice took her hand and gave it a squeeze as he nodded his head. "I'm going to take everyone home, and then I'm coming back to your house," he told her. "I'll see you in a bit."

When Brice arrived at her house later that evening, Misty had two cups of hot coffee on the kitchen counter and a scatter of papers on the table.

"What's all this?" he asked as he grabbed the coffee creamer from her refrigerator.

"Notes I've been taking since Tori was kidnapped," Misty replied. She'd pulled her hair up into a high, messy ponytail, and she stood over the papers, staring intently down at them as if they held some vital clue she might have missed.

"Wow, you've jotted down quite a few notes," Brice stated as he joined her at the table.

"There's something off here, don't you think?" Misty asked as she absently twirled a strand of hair around her forefinger.

Blowing into his steaming cup, Brice looked at her and asked, "What do you mean?"

Misty crossed her arms and shook her head. "Nothing really adds up," she replied. "Why did the kidnapper go to all the trouble to lure Tori to the hardware store in the first place? Why not take her from her home or even the coffee shop?"

Brice thought it over for a moment. "I don't know," he finally replied. "He definitely took a risk going to the store like that because I could have been there with Pops or stopped by at any time."

"Exactly. And why risk sneaking into Patrick Donovan's restaurant to put that note in with the trivia questions?"

Sipping on his coffee, Brice walked slowly around the table as he thought. "It definitely seems like he enjoys taking risks," he said after a moment. "It was also pretty dangerous for him to snatch Anna Douglas from the vet clinic right in the middle of the day like that."

"It wasn't very risky to grab me out of my backyard, though, when no one else was around," Misty muttered, her brow wrinkled in confusion.

Brice stopped dead in his tracks and nearly dropped his coffee cup over Misty's statement. "*What?*" he all but choked.

Oh, dear, I forgot to mention that I was also kidnapped, Misty thought with an inward moan.

"That's why I was at the vet this morning," she replied. "Some man shot poor Wally with a tranquilizer and then threw me into the back of his trunk..."

Slamming his cup down, Brice hurried around the table to grab Misty by the arms. "Misty, why on earth am I just now hearing about this?" he demanded, his face ashen. "Are you alright? Did he hurt you? How did you manage to escape?"

Gently removing her arm from his death grip, Misty patted Brice's hand and said, "I'm fine. Some stranger interrupted things and took the kidnapper away, leaving me to fend for myself. Thankfully, Theo was driving by and picked me up."

His eyes searching her face, he asked once again, "So, you're okay, then?"

Misty smiled softly and nodded. "Yes, I'm fine. Thankfully, Wally is, too."

As she went to kneel beside her pet and gently

rub him behind the ears, Brice frowned and asked, "All of this happened, and you didn't see the kidnapper's face? What about your security cameras outside?"

With a sigh, Misty said, "He put a bag over my head, so I couldn't see his face. And my cameras haven't been working for the last few weeks because they need new batteries."

Rolling his eyes, Brice asked drolly, "What good are security cameras if you let them die?" Shaking his head, he added, "Do you have any batteries here? If so, let's go change them right now."

After digging around a few of her kitchen drawers, Misty found the batteries and went outside with Brice. Thankfully, it was still light enough out that they didn't need a flashlight, and Misty held the ladder for Brice as he changed the batteries.

"Hey, why was Mr. Donovan at your house earlier when I called?" Brice suddenly asked as he was finishing up.

Misty blinked in surprise. "Oh, good Lord," she moaned, covering one side of her face with her hand.

"What's wrong?" Brice asked, quickly looking around as if expecting to see an intruder lurking about the grounds.

Misty had forgotten all about Patrick Donovan's visit. How could she forget something like that? Had the news been so traumatic that she'd simply blocked it all out?

Noticing how pale she'd suddenly become, Brice climbed down from the ladder and touched her arm. "What is it, Misty? Did he say something to upset you?"

Misty blew out a short, mirthless laugh as an unexpected flood of tears began to sting her eyes. "He sure did," she replied in a hoarse tone. Rubbing her temple, she added softly, "He said he's my father."

Brice's mouth dropped open. "***What?***"

He was looking at her like she'd lost her mind, which wasn't far from the truth. She felt like she might lose it at any moment.

Stepping away from him, Misty began to pace around the yard, wringing her hands. "Do you remember when I told you that the DNA website had found my father?" she asked. When Brice nodded, she continued, "Well, apparently it's Patrick Donovan; he and I share fifty percent DNA. Can you believe it?"

Brice slowly shook his head, dumbfounded. "But how?" he wanted to know.

Misty shrugged. "I don't know. Before he could explain, you called about Anna and I took off." Wrapping her arms around her waist, she went back to stand before Brice and said softly, "I never expected it to be this way, Brice. I never expected my father to be someone I'd known for several months. Patrick *knew* I came here searching for answers about my mother, and he acted as if he'd barely known her. How could he do that? I feel so overwhelmed with everything that's happening right now."

Pulling her into his arms, Brice rested his chin on top of her head and said gently, "I know, Misty. It'll be okay, though, I promise. Just take it one day at a time and try not to judge him too harshly until he's had a chance to fully explain. I've always had a lot of respect for Patrick Donovan, and I believe he's a good man.

Misty let him hold her for a moment, and the sound of his heart beating against her ear was comforting. Once she felt a bit more in control of her emotions, she pulled back and wiped her eyes.

"Once we find Tori," she said softly, "maybe I can think more clearly. Until then, though, I just can't deal with anything else."

Tugging on her hand, he began heading back inside the house as he said, "Let's get back to those notes then and see what we can figure out. We're going to find her, Misty. I know we will."

Swallowing past the lump in her throat, Misty followed him inside and whispered, "I pray you're right."

CHAPTER 14

Tori
Thursday morning

Tori's calves were cramped and her ankle was aching. She'd paced around her small room all night, worrying about Anna and who would be kidnapped next. Why hadn't he grabbed Misty? Had he done something else to her instead? Tori felt sick to her stomach, and when the door to her room opened the next morning, she wanted to fling herself at him and fight her way out, but she was just too tired.

"Hungry?"

He wore the mask again but thankfully kept his distance. She kept hers, as well, just in case he tried to attack her again. Would she be able to ward off another attack? She wasn't sure if she was strong enough.

"Is this food drugged, too?" she heard herself ask.

He lowered the tray to the floor and shook his head. "No," he replied. "If you try to escape again, though, your next meal will be."

As he began backing out of the door, Tori took a step forward and asked in a desperate tone, "How many more women are you going to kidnap?"

He paused, and she could feel the weight of his stare upon her through the darkness. "As many as I want," was his simple reply.

With those words, he slipped from the room and left just as quickly as he'd come moments before. Walking forward, Tori pressed her ear against the door and listened as he entered Anna's room. She could hear the poor girl crying and begging him to let her go, but surprisingly enough, he never spoke a word to her. Once he was gone, all that echoed throughout the building were Anna's haunting cries and the whisper of the wind.

Misty

Brice had stayed at Misty's house until almost midnight the night before, going over the notes with her. When she woke up the next morning, she felt like she'd been run over by a train. After fixing herself an extra large cup of coffee, though, she began to perk up.

As she ate her ham and cheese omelet, Misty searched for Kyra Kirby's boyfriend, Samuel, on social media. He was fifty-four and had apparently gone through a pretty nasty divorce nearly a year ago. According to his ex-wife, he was a lousy father and had been an abusive husband.

Sitting back in her chair, Misty drew one knee up to her chin and thought about what a nice person Kyra was. Why had she gotten involved with someone like Samuel? Misty knew everyone in town had been whispering about Kyra moving on so soon after her first husband's death a few months ago. Was she on the rebound and not thinking clearly? Or was Samuel's ex-wife simply exaggerating?

Pulling up her messaging app, Misty texted Dylan and said, *"Sorry to bother you, but I have a quick question. Do you know why Samuel Larson moved to Shady Pines?"*

It took nearly fifteen minutes for Dylan to answer her, and when he finally did, Misty had finished eating and was cleaning up the kitchen.

"He's from South Carolina, and he moved here because he knew Kyra in college and the two reconnected after his divorce," was his reply.

"Do you know much about him?" Misty asked.

"Only that he worked for the sheriff's office in Charleston and took a pay cut to move here. Oh, and according to him, his ex-wife is a witch of a woman and he's glad to finally be with someone as wonderful as Kyra. Why do you ask?"

Misty hesitated and chewed on her lip in thought. Finally, she replied, *"I saw him at the clinic last night without Kyra and I was just curious to know more about him. Did you ask him why he lied to Sheriff Ward about that report?"*

Misty's app showed that Dylan began to type, and then he erased it all. Nearly five minutes later, he finally responded with, *"Samuel said he never told Sheriff Ward I'd taken the report home, so I guess that was just a misunderstanding. As for the shoe print, it's pretty generic and won't do us any good until we manage to find a suspect."*

Pretty generic? A military-style hiking boot? Misty wanted to voice that question to Dylan but knew she couldn't since she'd promised Harris.

Just then, another text came through from Dylan.

"I ran the license plate number of the car you gave me," he stated. *"The car was reported stolen from Cloud Haven three days ago."*

With a sigh, Misty simply sent him a thumbs-up and locked her phone. It seemed that every lead ended up being a dead end, and she was feeling more and more frustrated. After a moment of deliberation, she went into her bedroom, got dressed, and headed into town with Wally in tow. She wanted to visit Kyra at the vet to ask questions about Samuel, and she also wanted to make certain Wally was still doing okay.

When Misty arrived at the clinic, Kyra was just putting the "open" sign on the door. After securing Wally's leash, Misty went inside and immediately noticed how worn the veterinarian looked.

"Kyra, are you okay?" Misty asked in a worried tone.

Rubbing her bloodshot eyes, Kyra nodded and said, "I'm okay, just worried sick about Anna." Glancing uncertainly around the large waiting room, she added, "I'm also a little nervous about being here, but I know the kidnapper wouldn't come after me, too."

Misty reached out and gently touched Kyra's arm. "You should still be careful," she cautioned the older woman. "It's still too soon to know exactly who this guy is after."

Shivering, Kyra pulled a little vial of pepper spray from her coat pocket and said, "That's why I have *this*; it helps me to feel a little more safe." Looking down at Wally, she asked, "How is he feeling? He's not acting sick or anything, is he?"

"He seems a little tired, but that's it," Misty replied. "I thought it would be best to let you check him out, though. Just to make sure."

Kyra nodded and led them into one of the examination rooms. While she checked Wally, Misty sat down and casually asked about Samuel.

"I heard the two of you met during college," she stated.

Kyra nodded, causing her messy red bun to flounce back and forth. "That's right," she replied. "After his divorce, he contacted me. Glenn had only been gone a couple of months, but I was grateful for the distraction. One thing led to another, though, and he decided to move here last month."

"Does he have any children?" Misty asked, although she already knew the answer to that question.

"He has two daughters, but his ex-wife has poisoned them against poor Sam," Kyra said with a disapproving *tsk*. "So, he rarely sees or even talks to them."

"What a shame," Misty replied. "I saw him here last evening while the police were investigating the crime scene and wondered where you were."

"Oh, you stopped by?" Kyra asked as she shined a light into Wally's eyes. "I guess I shouldn't be surprised; Sam said half the town was here." Putting away the light, she shook her head and sighed heavily. "I was just too shaken up to be here, so Sam made certain I got to my home safely and then came back to see if they would find anything."

So, they're not living together, Misty thought, wondering where Sam **did** live.

"Well, Wally seems to be just fine to me," Kyra announced, breaking Misty's thoughts.

"Oh, wonderful," Misty replied with a breath of relief. "Thanks so much, Kyra. Let me know if you hear any updates on Anna."

"I will, hon," Kyra replied with a wave as Misty led Wally back out to her car.

During the drive home, Misty kept thinking about Samuel and wondered if she should have asked Kyra where he was living. Would Kyra have balked at answering such a nosy question? Possibly so, and Misty made a mental note to ask Dylan about it once she got home.

Ten minutes later, Misty pulled up in front of her house and was surprised to see another car parked in the driveway. It was one she didn't recognize, and she didn't see anyone standing on her front porch. Feeling a little wary after what happened the day before, Misty grabbed her Taser gun from the glove compartment, and with a firm grip on Wally's leash, climbed from the car.

The area surrounding Misty's house was quiet, and even Wally seemed to sense something strange. His ears were up and his eyes alert as he slowly looked around, sniffing the air, and Misty noticed that not even the birds were chirping among the pine trees. Just then, a slight bit of movement caught her eye, and she turned to find a large black dog standing at the corner of her house, staring at her. It didn't move a muscle or blink its golden eyes, and even Wally froze in place as the two stared silently at one another. Misty immediately thought of the lone black wolf she'd heard so much about during her stay in Dahlonega, but there were no wolves in this area. Were there?

Suddenly, a loud whistle sounded from the back of the house, and the dog immediately turned and disappeared in that direction. Holding tightly to Wally's leash, Misty quickly hurried after the dog. When she rounded the corner and spotted both the dog and its owner, her eyes widened in shock.

CHAPTER 15

Z aylie?" Misty asked in a surprised tone. With a bright smile, Zaylie Layne hurried in Misty's direction to give her a big hug. Smutti, her black German Shepherd, trailed along quietly behind her owner.

"I'm sorry to just pop in on you like this," Zaylie explained, watching carefully as Smutti and Wally sniffed at each other, "but I lost your number when my phone crashed a few months ago. When I heard what was going on here in Shady Pines, though, I just had to look you up."

Misty had first met Zaylie when she'd lived in Savannah a few years ago. Zaylie was downtown one day doing a demonstration with a couple of her search and rescue dogs, one of whom was Smutti. Her family owned one of the most renowned training facilities in America, and Misty had been fascinated while she watched and listened to the demonstration. Afterward, Misty struck up a conversation with Zaylie, and the two had instantly become friends. Since Zaylie was constantly on the move, taking Smutti to different locations to search for missing people, the two lost touch after Misty left Savannah and hadn't talked since.

"How did you find my house?" Misty wanted to

know.

"You know Smutti and I can find anyone," Zaylie replied, her green eyes sparkling. "It was easy this time, though. All I had to do was stop at the local market and ask where you lived."

Misty laughed. "Small towns make it hard for a person to hide."

Looping her arm through Misty's, Zaylie began leading her back around to the front of the house. "You weren't really trying to hide, though, were you?" she asked. "I mean, I know you normally don't stay in one place for very long, but I get the feeling you've settled down here."

"You're right," Misty replied with a smile. "I've finally found the answers I've been looking for... well, most of them anyway, and I've decided to stay here." Stopping in her tracks, Misty looked at Zaylie and asked, "Wait, what did you mean when you said you heard what was going on here?"

Tossing a lock of auburn hair over one shoulder, Zaylie pulled her phone from her pocket and said, "Some influencer posted about the kidnappings on social media, and now every county within a hundred miles is talking about it."

Zaylie held up her phone for Misty to see the post, and her eyes widened in surprise when she saw that it had been made by Penny only yesterday afternoon. Wasn't she supposed to be on vacation? Had she barely made it off the plane before Theo or someone from town told her about Anna?

"Is it as bad as it sounds?" Zaylie asked, her tone

heavy.

Misty nodded. "Yes," she replied, sitting down on her top porch step. "The first woman that was kidnapped is my best friend, Tori Barlow. The creep made a grab for me yesterday morning, but I managed to escape with the help of a stranger."

Zaylie's eyes widened. "Wow, Misty, this is serious. Do you know if the police have searched any abandoned buildings near town?"

Misty shook her head. "Not that I know of," she replied.

"In my experience, when a kidnapper takes more than one person, he'll keep them in an out-of-the-way place in case the police decide to search his home." Glancing at her watch, Zaylie added, "I'm flying to Colorado in about four hours; a young girl went missing two days ago during a hike with her family and they asked me to come help with the search. Since I have a little bit of time before I have to head to the airport, how about we do some investigating of our own?"

Misty nodded eagerly. "I'm game. What did you have in mind?"

Tapping her chin, Zaylie asked, "Are there any old, abandoned buildings in the area that you know of?"

Misty thought it over for a moment. "There's an old school between here and Cloud Haven that's no longer in use," she said. "It's a good distance off the main road and I don't think anyone ever goes out there."

Zaylie snapper her fingers. "That would be the perfect place for someone to hide out. Shall we head that way?"

Misty agreed and hurriedly led Wally through the house and into the kitchen. As she made certain he had enough water, she noticed how he sat and watched her with a pair of sad, soulful eyes. Apparently, he thought he was getting a new sister and wasn't happy about having to share the attention.

"Stop looking so worried," Misty told him with a laugh. "Smutti is just a visitor; she's not here to stay. We'll all be back later, and I'll give you some extra chicken with your supper."

As Misty and Zaylie drove toward the school, Misty called Dylan to ask if he'd like to join them. She knew Sheriff Ward wouldn't like her interference, and she wanted to be above board with Zaylie's plan to search the school.

"Hey, I'm checking out a lead over in Savannah right now," Dylan said as soon as he answered the phone. "Can I call you back later?"

"Have you found Julian Cooper?" Misty asked hopefully, knowing that Savannah was the last place Cooper had lived.

"I'm not sure yet," he stated. "Is everything okay there?"

"A friend and I are about to go by the old school building to see if anyone has been there recently," she told him. "I thought you'd like to meet us there, but since you're busy, I'll let you know if we find anything."

"Sure, sounds good."

Misty ended the call, uncertain of whether Dylan had understood what she was doing. Oh, well. If she and Zaylie found anything, she would simply call Sheriff Ward and let him know.

As Misty turned the car down the road that led to the school, she wondered about the lead Dylan said he had on Julian Cooper. She knew he'd been in contact with the Savannah police about Cooper since Tori's first attack, but they'd been unable to locate him. Had he tried sneaking back to his home for something? If so, Misty hoped they'd caught him, and if they did, she prayed he'd tell them where Tori and Anna were being held.

The old road leading to the school was rutted and bumpy. There were a few houses here and there, but the area was mostly barren and desolate. The only people still living here were reclusive and kept to themselves, and Misty only hoped they didn't shoot at visitors.

"I can't imagine living way out here," Zaylie stated with a slight shiver. "I guess the school mainly served the families in this area?"

Misty nodded. "I don't know much about it," she said, "but this land was owned by several families who were all farmers. As the years went by, the families grew and there was a need for a school, so one was built. About twenty years ago, though, it closed down because most of the family members had either moved away or died."

Leaning forward in her seat, Zaylie pointed to a break in the trees up ahead and asked, "Is that it?"

Glancing at her phone, which no longer had any service, Misty said, "I assume so."

The brick building sat around fifty yards off the road and was partially surrounded by trees. It was shaped like the letter L, with a larger section that jutted out to the side, which Misty assumed to be the cafeteria. As she turned down the driveway that led to the front door of the school, she wondered if they'd made a mistake by coming out here by themselves. With no cell service and no one around who would be willing to help them, Misty only hoped Dylan would know where to find them if something happened.

Misty parked her car and climbed out, eyeing the dilapidated old building with a bit of trepidation. While Zaylie got Smutti from the back seat, she walked up to the front door and peered in through the smudged glass.

"Are you ready?"

Turning to look at her friend, Misty's eyes widened when she saw a gun in Zaylie's hand.

"I never go into a dangerous situation unprepared," Zaylie stated when she saw the look of surprise on Misty's face. Holding out a flashlight for Misty to take, she added, "Will you carry this?"

Nodding, Misty followed Zaylie as her friend opened the front door and carefully stepped inside. Smutti entered with her handler and stood quietly by her side, waiting for any commands.

"I don't see or hear anything," Zaylie said in a low voice. "Keep the flashlight beam out in front, and Smutti will alert us if anyone is here." Looking down at her dog, whose ears had perked up at the mention of her name, she commanded, "Smutti, search."

The dog immediately put her nose to the ground and began to slowly and calmly make her way through the front room. Smutti was one of the best SAR dogs in America. She'd been specially trained in both the trailing and air scent techniques, something not many dogs could do, and had successfully located dozens of missing people. She was Zaylie's personal dog and wouldn't work with any other handler; the special bond between dog and owner was obvious to anyone who saw them together. Misty had never actually seen Smutti at work, though, and watching her now caused her admiration and fascination for the profession to grow even stronger.

As Smutti sniffed around the room, Misty and Zaylie followed, their eyes searching for any signs of life. Other than a large desk which sat against one wall, the room was otherwise empty, and it didn't take Smutti long to make her way out into a long hallway. Misty shined the beam around, taking in all the doors on either side of the corridor, which she assumed to be classrooms. Cobwebs hung from the ceiling, and dirt and trash was scattered all along the floor.

Smutti had just made her way to the first

room when she suddenly stopped. She raised her nose from off the floor and sniffed the air, then smelled the doorframe. Misty's entire body tensed as she waited to see what had caught the dog's attention. She glanced at Zaylie, who was carefully and quietly watching her dog. When Smutti put her nose back to the ground and entered the room, Zaylie didn't seem at all surprised.

The small room was filled with old-fashioned desks and metal chairs. A whiteboard hung at an angle on the front wall, while school books and papers lay all along the floor. Smutti smelled around for a moment but soon moved on to the next room.

On and on they went, searching all the rooms and coming up empty. They were nearing the last room at the end of the hall, and Misty realized with surprise that this door was closed. Smutti approached the door more slowly this time, her movements calm but cautious. The moment she sniffed at the door, however, her whole body tensed and she began to prance around in circles. Misty found it odd that she didn't bark or make any sound, but by the way Zaylie quickly raised her gun and moved forward, she knew Smutti had found something.

Someone was on the other side of that door.

CHAPTER 16

Zaylie made a quick signal with her hand, and Smutti immediately came to stand at her side. As she slowly walked toward the door, she looked at Misty and whispered, "Give me the flashlight and stay behind the doorframe."

In all her years of doing dangerous, crazy things, Misty had never been more frightened. If the kidnapper really was on the other side of that door, he could kill Tori and Anna before Misty and Zaylie could stop him. What if they were too late, though? What if the two women were already dead?

With a steady hand, Zaylie grasped the doorknob and slowly turned the handle. In one swift movement, she threw the door open and peered around the doorframe. She held the flashlight underneath the gun, but Misty was standing too far back to see inside the room.

"I don't see anything," Zaylie whispered.

Suddenly, Smutti began to growl, and Misty felt the hair on the back of her neck rise. Before she could take a deep breath, the large silhouette of a man bounded from the room, nearly knocking the gun and flashlight from Zaylie's hand.

"Hold it, or I'll shoot!" Zaylie yelled.

With her heart in her throat, Misty watched as

the man skidded to a halt and slowly turned to face them. His face and clothes were covered in dirt, and his eyes were filled with fear as he stared into the bright beam of the flashlight.

"I-I ain't doin' no harm," he stammered.

Smutti was barking ferociously, but immediately stopped when Zaylie gave her the signal. She remained standing, however, her whole body tense and ready to defend her owner if need be.

"Who are you?" Zaylie demanded, the gun still pointed at the man.

"My name is Billy," he said, his voice trembling. "Billy O'Hadley. I-I live here."

Misty blinked in surprise, and as she carefully studied the man, she realized he was actually no older than sixteen. His face was filled with fear, and it looked like he hadn't eaten in days; by the smell emanating from his clothes, he also apparently hadn't bathed in several days either.

"Why are you living here?" Zaylie questioned as she slowly lowered the gun.

Rubbing his runny nose, Billy looked down at the floor and muttered, "Cuz my dad threw me out a few weeks ago. I thought I'd hide out here for a little while, and then maybe he'd let me come back home."

Misty and Zaylie looked at each other then, and it was obvious they were both thinking the same thing. Although Billy may have been sixteen or seventeen, he apparently had the mind of a child.

As he shuffled his feet awkwardly in the hallway, Misty's heart went out to him. She couldn't imagine how his father could be so cruel as to kick him out and force him to fend for himself.

"Billy, have you seen anyone else out here?" Misty asked him. Pulling out her cell phone, she found a picture of Tori and held it up for him to see. "We're looking for this woman. She's a very dear friend of mine, and she was kidnapped earlier this week."

Billy shook his head. "No, ma'am, I ain't seen no one. Ain't nobody brave enough to come out here. Except for the both of you."

"Well, if you happen to see anything suspicious, would you call me and let me know?" Misty asked as she wrote down her number on a piece of paper. Handing it to him, she asked, "You do have access to a phone, don't you?"

Billy looked at her like she was crazy. "Of course, I got a phone," he stated, shoving her number into his pocket. "My dad does, anyway."

With a smile, Zaylie said, "Thank you for your help, Billy. Now why don't you go on home to your father? You shouldn't be living out here."

Relieved to get away from the two crazy females with the dog, Billy spun on his heel and high-tailed it out of there.

"Well, that was…interesting," Zaylie stated with a chuckle once he was gone. Glancing down at Smutti, she said, "We're not used to quite so much action. Are we, girl?"

Smutti wagged her tail and nudged Zaylie's hand with her nose. As Zaylie lovingly rubbed the dog's ears, Misty wondered about her statement. From what she remembered about their conversations in the past, Zaylie had plenty of experience with this sort of thing. Her older sister, Zoe, was kidnapped when the girls were young, and Zoe was found several months later, murdered. The man responsible was never captured. Misty knew that training her dogs and going on search and rescue missions kept Zaylie busy, but she'd always managed to make time to research serial killer and kidnapping cases. Had she decided to give up on finding her sister's killer?

Before Misty could think of a polite way to ask, Zaylie said, "Let's finish our search here and then move on to the next place. Okay?"

Misty nodded and followed her friend through the rest of the building. When nothing was found, they went back to Misty's car and drove away. As they left the desolate and almost depressing area, Misty thought again of Billy and hoped that his father would let him come back home.

They'd no sooner made it back out on the main road when Zaylie's phone began to chime.

"Apparently, someone has been trying to get hold of me while we didn't have any signal," she muttered as she unlocked her phone. As she read the messages, she moaned, "Oh, no."

Misty glanced over at her and asked, "What's wrong?"

"It looks like my original flight got delayed until tomorrow, but there's another flight leaving from Atlanta in a little over five hours," she replied with a sigh. "If I'm going to make that flight, I've got to leave now. I'm sorry, Misty."

Misty nodded. "Don't worry, Z. I'll keep looking on my own." Glancing in the rearview mirror at Smutti, she added with a smile, "I won't have a specially trained dog to help me, though."

After slightly breaking the speed limit, Misty made it back to her place in record time. While Zaylie ran inside for a moment, Misty sat on the porch and watched as Smutti sniffed around the yard. Once she was finished, the large dog came and sat quietly next to Misty.

"What a good girl," Misty said softly as she rubbed Smutti behind the ears. She was so different from Wally, who was energetic, fun-loving, and eager to explore his surroundings. Smutti, on the other hand, was sweet and quiet and calmly observed everything around her. She missed nothing, and when she looked at you, it felt as if she could see right into your soul.

"Okay, I'm ready," Zaylie stated as she hurried out of the front door.

Smutti immediately stood and hurried to her owner's side. As Zaylie let the dog jump into the back seat of her car, she turned to Misty and said, "Be careful searching for your friends on your own, Misty. It can be very dangerous. Take a weapon with you, and a good flashlight."

Pulling her friend into a quick hug, Misty said, "Okay. Thank you so much for your help, Zaylie. Drive safely, and I'll text you my new number."

After Zaylie left, Misty went into the house. Wally greeted her like she'd been away for weeks, and she realized he was happy the other dog was gone.

"You're just a wee bit spoiled, aren't you, boy?" she asked him with a giggle as she scratched his back.

After texting her number to Zaylie as promised, Misty grabbed a blank sheet of paper, sat at the kitchen table, and began writing down all of the other abandoned buildings she knew about in the area. Once she was finished, she texted Brice, hoping he'd be able to go with her. He texted back moments later to say he'd taken Pops to Savannah for a doctor's appointment and wouldn't be back until later that afternoon. She then texted Dylan to ask about the Julian Cooper lead, but he never answered. After a few moments of deliberation, Misty grabbed her purse and Taser gun and headed back out to start searching. Dylan supposedly knew what she was doing, and it wouldn't hurt to help the local police a bit, would it? After all, the clock was ticking, and Misty couldn't just continue sitting idly by while Tori and Anna were at the mercy of this man.

CHAPTER 17

With the list in her purse, Misty went into town to Raymond's Hunting Supply to buy a few things she thought she might need. At the store, she grabbed a nicer flashlight than the one she had at home, a first aid kit, and a folding pocket knife. As she waited in the checkout line behind a rather talkative, older gentleman, she was so engrossed in her own thoughts that she didn't see Adam Dawson step up beside her.

"Going hunting?"

Blinking in surprise, Misty turned to see that Adam was inspecting the items she held with a curious look in his eyes.

"Oh, uh, something like that," she stammered.

Looking at her suspiciously, Adam asked, "Just what are you up to, Misty?"

The older gentleman finally moved on, and Misty stepped up to the cashier and handed him the items she wanted to purchase.

"Who says I'm up to anything?" she asked Adam with a mysterious smile. "Besides, what are *you* doing at a hunting supply store in the middle of the day? Shouldn't you be working?"

"I got off work early today and stopped by to grab an old gun my dad had repaired. Now, young lady, why don't you answer *my* question?"

As Misty paid the cashier, she considered confiding in Adam. He'd helped out before with her crazy ideas, hadn't he? Perhaps he would again this time. Plus, it wouldn't hurt to have someone around to help, just in case she found something.

Just as she was about to ask him to join her outside so she could explain, the store owner stepped from the back room with Adam's gun in tow. Misty knew Mr. Raymond would talk poor Adam's ears off, and before he had the chance to catch her, too, she waved goodbye and hurried out of the store.

Misty drove a couple of miles outside of the city limits and turned down a narrow road that led to the town's old fairgrounds. The area had once been a popular place for many activities, including town picnics, Fourth of July fireworks, and even the circus a few times. It hadn't been used in years, and Misty only learned about it recently from the Barlows. They told her there was a large building on the property with a carousel, arcade, small theater, and food court. There were rumors around town that restoration plans were in the making, but for now, it was abandoned and no one was supposed to go near the place. A handmade wooden gate barred the entrance to the road, but it was easy enough to move aside. Misty thought that such an area would be an ideal place for a kidnapper to keep his victims.

The small, narrow road leading to the

fairgrounds was overgrown and bumpy. Thick trees lined either side, making the day seem darker than it actually was. When Misty rounded a corner and saw the clearing up ahead, she knew she was almost there and pulled her car to the side. Grabbing the small backpack she'd brought with her, she filled it with the items she'd purchased at the hunting supply store, along with her cellphone and Taser gun.

"Here goes nothing," she muttered under her breath as she climbed from the car and headed down the road.

Birds chirped among the trees, making the dark, overgrown area seem almost cheerful. Misty kept her eyes peeled for any movement among the thick woods, but everything remained still and peaceful. When she reached the clearing, she stopped for a moment and took it all in. Nearly one hundred acres of overgrown grass sprawled out before her, the empty picnic tables and open pavilions that dotted the barren landscape testifying to what was once a place filled with laughter and families. The large building the Barlows told her about sat in the center of it all, and Misty studied it carefully, looking for any signs of life. It sat there, still and quiet, with its broken windows and peaked roof. Misty saw no one about, but there were clear signs that someone had been here recently because there were lines in the weeds and grass where a vehicle had recently driven.

Taking a deep breath, Misty walked across the

grounds until she reached the massive building. She peered through a few of the windows first, and when she saw no movement inside, she pulled open one of the side doors and stepped inside.

The building was dark and eerily quiet. Taking the flashlight from her backpack, Misty shined it around what apparently was once the food court. Empty chairs and tables still lined the room, and Misty felt that if she really tried, she could hear echoes of voices and laughter from the past.

Slowly, she began to walk around the room, shining her flashlight into each section where individual food vendors would have been. Finding nothing, she moved on toward a massive archway just ahead and pushed open two heavy double doors. Peering inside, she discovered a small theater with about sixty or so chairs set up before a large projection screen. She walked slowly and quietly around the dark room, shining her light down each aisle and between the chairs.

Maybe this was a dumb idea, she thought, sighing inwardly as she left the theater empty-handed and went back out into the food court.

She was walking toward another archway that seemed to lead into another section of the building when she suddenly heard an odd sound. There was a slight creaking noise coming from the other side of the room. Was it a door opening? Then the sound of footsteps echoed throughout the room, and Misty froze, her heart pounding.

Stepping quietly into the shadows, Misty clicked

off her flashlight and frantically searched for her cell phone. When she found it, she unlocked the screen and started to call Dylan, but stopped when she realized she had no reception.

She was on her own.

The footsteps were drawing nearer, and Misty knew she would be spotted standing against the wall, barely amongst the shadows. She couldn't see anyone, so she took her chances and hurried on toward the other section of the building, hoping she would be able to find an exit. Thankfully, she'd thought to wear sneakers, and her shoes barely made any sound.

Misty rounded the corner into the third section and stopped, caught off guard by what stood just on the other side. A massive, shadowy silhouette of horse hooves, gaping eyes, and bared teeth rose up before her. Normally, she found carousels to be endearing, but the way the shadows drifted along the angles of the frozen, wooden expressions made her unease grow even more.

The footsteps suddenly began to move faster, and with a catch of her breath, Misty hurried onto the old platform and crouched down behind one of the galloping horses. She sat as still as possible, her heart pounding, and thought that if the carousel suddenly lit up and started moving, she'd die right then and there of sheer fright.

A tall, dark figure rounded the corner Misty had just moved away from. It stopped, as if listening or waiting for something to happen, and Misty squinted through the shadows, trying to see who the man was. Suddenly, he turned and looked right at her, shining a bright light directly into her face.

CHAPTER 18

Misty gasped in surprise, tumbling backward with a loud *umph!*

"Misty?" a low voice echoed out, and the shadow quickly hurried toward her.

"Adam, what on earth are you trying to do?" Misty asked in a breathless tone. "Scare me half to death?"

Offering her a hand, Adam pulled Misty to her feet and said, "What am *I* doing? What are *you* doing?"

Stepping off the carousel platform, Misty dusted off her rear end and said, "A friend told me that kidnappers often keep their victims in out-of-the-way places, so I thought I'd check out a few of our local, abandoned buildings."

Adam stopped in his tracks and looked at Misty like she'd just grown a second head. "Misty, have you lost your mind?" he scolded her. "Why would you do something like that? And what exactly did you plan to do if *this* is where he was keeping them?"

Misty pulled the Taser gun from her bag and showed it to him. "I planned to use this."

Shaking his head, Adam said, "Yeah, like *that* would have done you any good just now if *I'd* been the kidnapper."

Misty bit her lip sheepishly. "You're right. I should have had it in my hand instead of in my bag."

Rolling his eyes, Adam said matter-of-factly, "No, you shouldn't have been doing something so crazy in the first place."

"Adam, I've got to do **something,**" she stated, planting her hands on her hips. "The police don't seem to be doing such a great job of finding Tori and Anna, or of stopping this guy from kidnapping again. I just thought I would help a little."

With a sigh, Adam touched her on the arm and said, "I understand, but at least take someone with you next time, okay? I mean, you could have shared your plans with me earlier and I would have gladly come along."

Shoving the Taser gun back into her bag, Misty began walking through the large arcade-type room. "I was going to tell you," she said, "but I knew once Mr. Raymond caught you..." Stopping, she turned to look back at Adam and asked, "Hey, how *did* you get away from Mr. Raymond and find me here?"

"I'm afraid I was a bit rude trying to get away from him before you left," he replied with a sheepish grin. "But I managed to keep an eye on which direction you went and followed you."

"Look at you, being sneaky," Misty said with a chuckle as she shined her light around the room.

"I knew you were up to something, and I just wanted to make sure you were safe," Adam said.

Touching her arm again, he added in a warm tone, "I know you're used to doing everything alone, but with a kidnapper on the loose, I didn't want anything to happen to you."

Misty stopped and looked up at him, feeling the intensity of his gaze through the shadows. She immediately thought of how he'd been there for her when she'd discovered what happened to her mother, and the tender way in which he'd kissed her. He was such a good person, with a heart as big as an ocean, and Misty knew any girl would be lucky to have him.

Before Misty could gather her thoughts, Adam looked away, breaking the spell, and asked, "So, you and Brice...are the two of you...?"

Misty's heart caught at the unasked question, and she felt as if she were standing at a very important crossroads. The only thing was, she didn't know which way to go and she knew that now wasn't the time to make any decisions about her feelings.

"I don't really know," she replied with a sigh. "Brice and I haven't had a chance to talk things out yet."

Whether or not she knew what was in her heart, she wanted to be open and honest with Adam. He at least deserved that.

Adam nodded understandingly. "Well, once all of this is over, maybe you and I could talk?" he asked.

"Sure," she replied with a smile.

They continued to search the remainder of the building but found nothing. As they headed back out to their cars, Adam asked if there were any other places she wanted to search.

"Yes, I have several places in mind," she replied.

"Let's go check them out now," he told her. "If you'd like, you can leave your car here and we can just take my truck."

After pulling her car back up closer to the main road, Misty locked it, grabbed her list, and climbed into Adam's truck. The second place they visited was an old hunting cabin back in the woods. Pops had told Misty about it once; apparently, the cabin was originally built in the 1800s and used by many of the town's founding fathers. The last owner died over five years ago, so the place was in shambles, but Misty still wanted to check it out.

"I haven't been back here in ages," Adam commented as he drove down the bumpy dirt road that led to the cabin.

Misty looked at him in surprise. "You've been here before?"

Adam nodded. "Sure," he replied. "Mr. Nixon, the previous owner, would let Dad and me use it when we'd go hunting."

After driving over two miles, the cabin finally came into sight. It was larger than Misty thought it would be, and even though she could tell it had been renovated throughout the years, it still had that old pioneer look to it. There didn't seem to be any life around, though, except for a few rabbits hopping frantically away and several squirrels scurrying into the trees. As soon as Misty climbed from the truck, she knew they'd hit another dead end.

"We can look around," she said with a sigh, "but it's obvious no one has been here in ages."

Misty and Adam poked their heads inside the musty old place, taking in all the cobwebs and dust that looked to be several inches thick. The floorboards creaked beneath their feet, as if speaking of how lonely the place had been for company, and just for a moment, Misty let her imagination run wild. She could picture the town's founding fathers, gathered around the table as they played a game of cards in the glow of a lantern. She wished with fervency that places like this could talk. Oh, of the stories that would be told!

"Ready?" Adam asked, touching Misty's shoulder.

Feeling disappointed at finding yet another dead end, Misty nodded and followed Adam back out to his truck without a word. As they drove away, Misty rolled her window down and stared at the cabin as it drifted further and further away, as if retreating back into the past.

Once back out on the main road, they headed to the third stop. On the way there, they chatted about Misty's trip to Dahlonega, and she told him about Patrick Donovan. He was just as shocked as Brice had been and wanted to know when Misty planned to talk to Mr. Donovan again.

"Once we find Tori, I feel like I'll be more ready to talk to him," she replied, watching as fields of green grass and cows whirled by. "Hey, don't say anything about this, okay?"

Adam nodded, his eyes on the road ahead. "I won't," he promised.

As they drove further away from town, Misty noticed a large black SUV following them from a distance. It had appeared behind them shortly after they'd left the cabin and had seemingly been trailing them ever since. After a while, it turned down a side road, and Misty didn't think anything else about it.

"Where do I turn?" Adam asked.

Glancing at the map on her phone, Misty said, "You've still got a couple of miles to go, and then you'll turn to the left."

She'd no sooner gotten the words from her mouth when, suddenly, the same black SUV shot out in front of them from a road on Misty's right. With a gasp, she clutched the door handle as Adam swerved to miss the vehicle. His tires squealing, he fought to maintain control of his truck, but it was no use. They spun wildly about as everything around them became a blur. Her heart pounding, Misty squeezed her eyes shut and clenched her teeth tightly, feeling every jerk and bump of the truck as it veered off the road and into the nearby ditch. For a moment, she feared they were going to flip, but almost as soon as it all started, they slammed to a stop and everything was deathly silent.

CHAPTER 19

Misty slowly opened her eyes and looked toward Adam, her head swimming. His face was blurry and he seemed to be bobbing oddly back and forth, but then she realized the dizziness was simply causing her to see double.

"Are you okay?" Adam asked, and through the haze, Misty saw him reach for her.

"Y-yes." She nodded, taking his outstretched hand. "Did we hit the other guy?"

"No," Adam replied, gritting his teeth as he tried unsuccessfully to back his truck out of the ditch. With a sigh, he turned the truck off and forced his door open. "The idiot just went on his merry way like nothing happened. I wish I could have seen who it was or gotten his license plate number."

Unable to get out of her own door due to the passenger side of the truck being squished against a massive amount of kudzu, Misty crawled across the console and climbed from the truck with Adam's help.

"I'm pretty sure it was the same SUV I spotted following us earlier," Misty told him as they climbed out of the ditch.

Glancing at her in surprise, Adam asked, "You mean you think he did this on purpose?"

Misty nodded. "Yes. I think he followed us for a bit, then took a side road shortcut, which enabled him to get a bit ahead of us. Then, when he saw us coming, he intentionally ran us off the road."

Rubbing the back of his neck, Adam pulled his cell phone from his pocket and called Dylan. After explaining what happened, he said, "I think your truck can pull mine out of this ditch. You wouldn't happen to be close by, would you?"

"No, but an extra set of keys to my truck are in a magnetic box by the back left tire," Dylan told Adam, who had put the call on speakerphone. "Are you two okay? Do I need to send an ambulance out there?"

Adam glanced questioningly at Misty, and she shook her head.

"We're both fine," Adam said. "I'll call you if I need help getting my truck out."

When he ended the call, Misty asked, "Does Dylan live near here?"

Adam nodded toward the road the SUV had come from. "Yes, he lives about a half mile down that road," he replied, and the two began walking in that direction. "He has a really nice place; I did some electrical work for him when he first moved here."

It didn't take long for them to walk to Dylan's house, and as they neared what had once been an old farmhouse, Misty was surprised that Dylan lived so far out of town. The area, though, was beautiful. The two-story house had recently been painted, and the five acres of land were vibrantly green and well-kept. A massive F-250 was parked in a barn in the backyard, and as they stepped into the large structure, Misty immediately began poking around.

"Can't help that nosy side, can you?" Adam teased as he fished around the truck's back tire for the spare key.

"I prefer curious," she quipped in return.

The barn itself was obviously quite old, but Dylan had refurbished it nicely. All of his tools were very neat and tidy, and Misty spotted a corner filled with fishing gear.

"Apparently, our local detective enjoys catching a fish or two," Misty stated out loud.

"As if he ever has any time off to go fishing," Adam replied with a chuckle.

"Did you find the key?" Misty asked.

"Yeah, here it is," Adam grunted as he pulled the magnetic box from underneath Dylan's truck. "Now I need to make sure he has a towing strap."

While Adam searched for the strap, Misty walked over to the fishing corner to look at the cluster of photos Dylan had hanging on the wall. One was of Dylan when he was a little boy; he stood next to an older man and wore a big smile as he proudly held up a large fish dangling from a hook. The other photos were of Dylan and who Misty assumed to be a few of his military friends; they all stood on the bank of a huge lake, wearing waders and big grins. Dylan looked so relaxed and carefree in the photos that Misty wondered what had happened to make him become so serious.

"Okay, I'm ready," Adam called.

As Misty turned to walk back toward him, she stopped in her tracks when she suddenly heard a creak coming from above. Glancing up, she asked, "Adam, is there a second floor up there?"

Adam opened the driver's side door and said, "I think so; I'm pretty sure Dylan added it himself."

Misty heard another creak just then and hurried to Adam's side. "It sounds like someone is up there," she whispered, grabbing his arm.

Adam listened for a moment and then said with a laugh, "What you're hearing, Miss Raven, is squirrels. There's no way anyone is up there; Dylan just uses it for storage."

"Are you sure it's squirrels?" Misty asked uncertainly.

Adam patted her arm and nodded. "Yes," he assured her. "As an electrician, I've heard my fair share of attic squirrels."

Feeling better, Misty smiled and said, "I'm sure you're right."

As she walked around the truck to climb into the passenger seat, she spotted something resting in one of the darker, shadowed corners. Her eyes narrowing, she stepped closer and bent down to have a better look. There, squeezed between a shovel and a large box of ant killer, was a pair of military-style hiking boots. And the soles were covered in mud.

It took nearly thirty minutes for Adam to pull his truck out of the ditch, and once he was finished, they both were starving.

"We're not far from Cloud Haven," Adam said after they'd returned Dylan's truck. "Want to get some barbecue?"

Misty readily agreed, and twenty minutes later, they were driving through the tiny town that stirred so many emotions in Misty. As they drove past the old church where Misty's mother had left her as a child, she touched the locket that rested around her neck and sighed. After so many years of searching, it had been agonizingly painful for Misty finally to learn the truth of what had happened to her mother. She'd come to accept it these last few months, but it still hurt.

Once they arrived at the small restaurant in the center of town, it didn't take long to get their plates of steaming hot barbecue, baked beans, coleslaw, and cornbread. As they carried their food outside to one of the two tables by the street, Misty felt her stomach rumble.

"At least it's still nice enough outside to eat without dying of a heatstroke," Misty joked as the two sat down.

Adam laughed, nodding his head in agreement, and silence filled the space between them for a few moments as they dug into the delicious meal. As she took a sip of sweet tea, Misty glanced out at the street and was surprised to see Noah Welch coming out of the pharmacy.

"I wonder why he came to this pharmacy instead of the one in Shady Pines?" Misty asked.

Adam shrugged his broad shoulders. "Maybe he was visiting someone in town."

"Hi, Noah!" Misty called out.

Glancing across the street in surprise, Noah waved his hand and walked over to join them.

"What are you two doing here?" he asked.

By the look in his eyes, Misty immediately knew he was wondering why she was here with Adam when he'd just seen her with Brice a few nights before at *Pat's Kitchen.* He peered down at her disapprovingly, and although Misty wanted to defend herself, she chose to hold her tongue on the matter.

"We were out, uh, running some errands," Misty stammered, clearing her throat, "and decided we wanted some of this delicious barbecue. How about you?"

"Oh, I hate barbecue," he stated, although Misty felt he knew that was not what she'd meant. "It makes me sick to my stomach. There are a lot of foods, though, that do that to me. I have a very sensitive stomach."

When Misty and Adam just sat there, both trying to figure out how to respond, he turned to Adam and asked, "How is Lexi doing? I saw her the other day in town, but didn't get the chance to speak to her."

As the two men talked, Misty slowly leaned over to try to get a look inside the two shopping bags Noah held. The one facing her looked to be full of rubbing alcohol, Band-Aids, and Neosporin. She couldn't see what was inside the other bag, but she wondered why he needed so many first-aid supplies.

"Well, enjoy the rest of your lunch," Noah said, interrupting Misty's thoughts.

Waving goodbye, Misty watched as Noah's figure slowly faded away down the street. Once he was out of earshot, she turned to Adam and asked, "Are the two of you good friends?"

"Noah isn't good friends with anyone," he replied with a chuckle. "He's too much of an introvert."

Pushing aside her now clean plate, she rested her chin on her hand and asked, "Does he have any family?"

Adam leaned back in his chair, his black hair glistening in the afternoon sun. "His dad died when he was a baby, and his mom passed away last year."

"No grandparents? Siblings?"

When Adam shook his head, Misty immediately felt sorry for Noah. She knew what it was like to be all alone in the world and wished she'd made an effort to be nicer to him, rather than trying to figure out what was in those two shopping bags.

After throwing away their trash, Misty and Adam headed back out of town. They'd just passed

Mr. Joe Caddel's furniture store, where Misty had gotten several handmade pieces for her house. She was about to suggest they stop in and see him when her cell phone chimed.

"It's from Dylan," she stated out loud. "They went out to investigate the area where the SUV ran us into the ditch. He said they found some fresh tire tracks where a vehicle ran off the road and the tracks look the same as the ones found on Mr. Porter's property, behind the hardware store."

Raising his eyebrows, Adam said, "Wow. I really wish I'd been able to get that license plate number."

Chewing on her lip for a moment, she glanced at Adam uncertainly before finally breaking down and telling him about the boots she'd seen in Dylan's barn.

"He's ex-military," he replied with a shrug. "Of course, he has boots like that."

"True," Misty muttered. "Do you know much about him? I tried to ask about his background, but he clammed up on me."

"He seems to be a pretty private fellow," Adam replied. "I think he had some bad experiences in the military, which is probably why he doesn't like talking about himself."

Glancing at Adam in surprise, she asked, "How do you know that?"

"While I was working at his house, he had a visitor," Adam replied as he turned down the road where Misty had left her car. "I think the man used to be Dylan's commanding officer. Anyway, they went into the kitchen to talk, but I couldn't help overhearing part of their conversation. The man kept saying it wasn't Dylan's fault and that he shouldn't blame himself. After he left, Dylan came into the living room where I was working and just stared out the window. After a moment, he turned to me and said he was happy to have found such a beautiful, peaceful place out in the country. I got the impression he was glad to not have any close neighbors or people around to bother him."

As Misty unbuckled her seatbelt, she pondered Adam's words. She knew PTSD was a real thing and something a lot of people struggled with. Why then had Dylan chosen to become a detective? Perhaps he hadn't figured on having to solve many crimes in such a small town. Is that why he seemed to be dragging his feet on this case? He just wasn't up to doing the job?

"Thanks for everything today, Adam," she told him as she opened the passenger side door.

"What about those other places on your list?" he wanted to know.

"I plan to go tomorrow," she replied. "It's too late to go anywhere else today."

"Okay, I'll pick you up first thing in the morning," he replied with a twinkle in his eyes.

Smiling, Misty nodded and said, "Okay, if you insist. See you in the morning."

As Misty drove away, she decided there was one more place she'd like to visit before going home, and that was Tori's house. She had a hunch about something and wanted to check it out.

When she arrived at her friend's house thirty minutes later, it was beginning to get dark outside. She pulled into the driveway, grabbed her flashlight, and headed around to the back of the house. Bending over, Misty shone the flashlight around the backyard for nearly ten minutes. Mrs. Peterson had said she'd seen someone running from around the back of Tori's house, and...

There. When Misty found it, her eyes widened, and she crouched down to get a better look. In the dirt just beneath the kitchen window was a shoe print, and although she couldn't tell for sure, she was willing to bet it matched the one found in the woods behind the hardware store. The one of a military-style hiking boot.

Grabbing her cell phone, Misty snapped a picture of the shoe print and stood back up. She'd just shoved the phone back into her pocket when a twig suddenly snapped from behind and immediately she knew she was not alone. Before she could react, one hand roughly grabbed her around the arm while the other slapped over her mouth.

CHAPTER 20

Misty's heart pounded as the flashlight tumbled from her hand and rolled across the yard. Yanking her head to the side, she was able to get her mouth free and let out a loud, ear-piercing scream. The hand on her arm loosened a bit, and Misty swung an elbow back, striking a hard chest. With an *oomph,* he let her go, and Misty took off at a dead run.

"Oh, no you don't."

The words were angry and tense, and Misty could hear his feet striking hard against the ground as he pursued after her. The side of Tori's house was only a few feet away; if she could just make it before being caught again, perhaps one of the neighbors would see her and come over to help. He wasn't far behind, though; she could almost feel his fingers reaching out, only inches away from grasping hold of her hair or clothes.

Misty rounded the corner of the house like an antelope sprinting for its life as a ferocious lion charged from behind. She glanced frantically around for someone to help when a dark silhouette suddenly appeared out of nowhere only a few feet in front of her. With a gasp, Misty skidded to a stop, her heart catching in her throat. Had he gone the other way and was waiting for her to run right into him?

"What on earth is going on out here?"

Squinting through the darkness, Misty nearly collapsed with relief when she realized the silhouette belonged to Mrs. Peterson from across the street. Grabbing the old lady by the arm, Misty began pulling her away from the house.

"Th-there's a man chasing me," she panted. "We need to get out of here before he harms us both."

"Hayden?" Mrs. Peterson called out, stopping Misty. "Is that you? I didn't realize you were home yet."

Glancing over her shoulder, Misty saw the large figure of a man coming toward them from around the back of the house. He seemed to be out of breath as well, and through the darkness, Misty recognized Tori's newest neighbor.

"Yes, it certainly is," he snapped in annoyance.

Looking between the two of them, Mrs. Peterson asked, "What is going on?"

Suddenly, the street lights flicked on, and Misty could see the anger in Hayden's eyes as he glared at her.

"That's what I'd like to know," he stated. "What were you doing, sneaking around in Tori's backyard?"

Misty didn't care for the tone in Mr. Brownley's voice, and crossing her arms defensively, she said, "I was checking on something in *my* best friend's yard. What were *you* doing back there?"

"I stepped out on my back deck and saw

someone suspicious lurking around out here," he replied. Cocking an eyebrow, he added, "You should be thankful I handled it myself instead of calling the police on you."

"Do you often handle things yourself?" Misty asked with a sniff.

Hayden's jaw clenched, but before he could say anything, Mrs. Peterson cleared her throat and said, "Well, since I know everything is okay, I'm going back to finish watching my show. Good night, you two."

As Mrs. Peterson hurried back to her house, Misty and Hayden stood there awkwardly in silence. Finally, Misty decided to take the high road and said, "I should have come by tomorrow when it was daylight instead of tonight when it was so dark. I'm sorry if I scared you."

"You didn't scare me," Hayden retorted. "But yes, for your own good, you shouldn't be lurking around other people's houses at night. Even if you *are* used to doing things your own way."

With that being said, Hayden spun around on his heel and marched back to his own home. Bristling at the rebuttal, Misty stomped over to her car with a huff and slammed the door. She had to admit that she was surprised at Hayden's attitude; he'd seemed rather nice the other day when she'd bumped into him after Anna was kidnapped. Perhaps she really had scared him and he'd simply lashed out at her because of it.

It wasn't until she was driving away that she

suddenly wondered how Hayden Brownley knew enough about her to point out she liked to do things her own way.

When Misty arrived home, she stopped at her mailbox before turning down her driveway. After retrieving the mail, she closed the lid and drove down the dark, bumpy road that led to her house. Once she parked her car and climbed out, she stood for a moment and listened to the crickets. The sound was peaceful and relaxing, and she suddenly realized how exhausted she was. With a yawn, she grabbed her things and walked inside.

Turning on all the lights, she headed into the kitchen and tossed the mail on the counter. After letting Wally out, she began shuffling through the envelopes, which were mostly advertisements and a few bills. When she reached the bottom of the stack, however, her forehead wrinkled as she stared at the single piece of paper that was folded in two.

Slowly, Misty unfolded the paper, and her eyes widened when she recognized the same handwriting from the first note that was left on her front porch.

"I cannot punish you, my dear, for treading where you don't belong. Someone else will have to pay for the things that you've done wrong."

Misty's heart began to pound as she slowly sank

into a nearby chair. What did this note mean? Was it from the kidnapper, and he was angry that she was interfering? With trembling hands, she texted Dylan a photo of the note. Seconds later, he called her.

"Where did that note come from?" he wanted to know.

"It was in my mailbox when I got home just now," she told him. "Dylan, what does he mean by someone else will have to pay for what I've done wrong?"

Dylan sighed. "I don't know," he said. "Put the note in a bag just like you did with the first one and I'll stop by in the morning to pick it up. You need to watch your step, Misty. This guy is dangerous, and he's not happy that you're poking your nose where it doesn't belong."

Misty swallowed past the lump in her throat. What if someone got hurt because of her? What if he hurt Tori or…or worse? She was just trying to help, but what if she'd made the situation worse?

"I'll be looking for you in the morning," she told Dylan and then hung up.

Misty's stomach was in knots for the rest of the night. She tried to sleep but couldn't seem to relax. After a while, she got up and fixed herself a cup of chamomile tea. It was nearly two a.m. when she finally dozed off, but her sleep was restless and filled with disturbing dreams. Anytime she was upset, she always tended to dream of her mother, and tonight was no exception. The flashbacks returned with full force, and she was taken back to the last night she saw with her mother. She heard the tears in Elena's voice when she left Misty at the church and said goodbye. She could feel the gentle kiss against her cheek and smelled the soft scent that clung to her mother's clothes. When she finally woke up, tears soaked her pillowcase, and she sat up to look at the clock. It was a little after three in the morning, and Misty went into the bathroom to wash her face. Staring at herself in the mirror, she wondered if she'd ever stop having those dreams and flashbacks. She finally had answers now, and she was thankful for that, but it seemed that the night so long ago when she'd lost her mother would forever haunt her.

CHAPTER 21

The clock read six a.m., and Lexi Dawson was wide awake. As a full-time nurse, she was often up before sunrise, but she seemed to have a difficult time relaxing since her return home. With everything that was going on in her hometown, she found herself feeling nervous and on edge. Finally, at a few minutes past six, she threw back her covers and climbed out of bed. Perhaps a long, early morning run would help to burn off some nervous energy.

She slipped into her running clothes and tiptoed quietly downstairs so as not to awaken her parents. Her family lived out in the country, which meant the roads were quiet and peaceful and perfect for a run. She'd spoken to her brother, Adam, last night and planned to join him and Misty Raven later to search a few of the local abandoned buildings in the area. Glancing at her smartwatch, she saw that she had plenty of time to exercise before she needed to get ready for the outing.

The sun was barely beginning to lighten a drab, gray sky when Lexi began jogging down her parents' driveway. It was too dark for even the birds to be awake just yet, and crickets still sang their lullabies among the grass and bushes. The area was quiet and serene, and Lexi took a deep, cleansing breath. She normally played classical music through her earbuds when she ran, but she wanted to be more aware of her surroundings this time. Just in case.

As she picked up her pace and soaked in the fresh, cool morning breeze, she thought about Misty and wondered what was keeping her from dating Adam. Lexi liked Misty and would love to finally have a sister-in-law, and she knew Adam was crazy about her. So what was holding Misty back? Brice Barlow? That's what Adam said when she'd asked him about it, and even though Lexi loved her brother dearly, she could understand Misty's dilemma. Brice Barlow was what every woman's dreams were made of, including her own. But then again, she'd heard other women say the same thing about Adam, too. She only hoped her brother wouldn't get hurt.

Lexi got so lost in her thoughts that she roamed further away from her parents' house than she'd intended. When she suddenly heard the sound of an approaching vehicle, she stopped dead in her tracks. Who would be driving down their road so early in the morning? Had Adam decided to come by earlier than he'd originally said? She hadn't felt her phone vibrate in her pocket. Glancing at her smartwatch, she checked for any missed calls or messages but didn't see any.

Bright headlights rounded the corner just up ahead, and Lexi blocked her eyes from the blinding lights. The car stopped and just sat there for a brief moment as if staring at her. It was only about twenty feet away, but she couldn't see who it belonged to or who was driving. Feeling uneasy, Lexi was reaching into her back pocket for her phone when the driver's door suddenly opened and the large figure of a man stepped out. The headlights still kept her from identifying who it was, but Lexi knew she needed to get out of there. And fast.

Forgetting about the phone, she spun on her heel and made a mad dash back down the road toward her childhood home. She was athletic and quick on her feet, but he was much bigger and she knew she wouldn't stand much of a chance if he caught her.

Why did I go for a run by myself with a kidnapper on the loose? she thought as sweat dripped from her brow. He was pursuing after her; she could hear him panting from behind. She wanted to turn around and defend herself, but running was her best defense. If only she could get within view of her parents' home, maybe they would hear her scream.

Suddenly, the toe of Lexi's shoe connected with a small protruding root in the ground. With a gasp, she lunged forward and slammed onto the ground with such force that the air was knocked from her lungs. As she lay there, gasping for breath, his shadow fell over her and she knew with a sinking heart that the chase was over.

Misty

The morning seemed to dawn earlier than usual, but Misty was up before her clock alarmed. She always seemed to be able to process her thoughts better when she was working, so she got up early and started doing some work on the house before Adam arrived. Plus, there was no point in staying in bed when you couldn't sleep.

It was after seven o'clock when she heard Wally begin to whine to go outside. Taking off her work apron, Misty hurried downstairs to let him out. After a few moments, Wally ran over to the path that wound through the woods behind the property and turned to look at Misty hopefully. Thankful that he was feeling well enough to go for a walk, Misty happily obliged him.

Their walk through the woods was peaceful and quiet. The morning was gray and overcast, and it seemed that the whole world was still sleeping. Wally chased a stick up and down the path for what felt like a hundred times until Misty's arm felt like it might fall off.

"Come on, boy," she called to him as she turned back toward the house. "It's time you and I both ate some breakfast."

At the mention of food, Wally forgot all about

the stick and bounded after Misty. As they made their exit out of the woods a few moments later and neared the house, however, his excitement turned to wariness. His pace slowed, his tail lowered, and his ears bent backward as he began to sniff the air.

"What's wrong?" Misty asked him, her body tensing as she looked around. All she could think about was the man who tranquilized Wally and tried to kidnap her, and her mind automatically went into defense mode. Grabbing a nearby stick, she clutched Wally's collar firmly in her hand as the two carefully made their way up to the house.

When they were only a few feet away from the back porch, the sound of approaching footsteps could be heard coming from around the side of the house. Wally stopped, and facing the direction of the footsteps, began to growl.

"Who's there?" Misty called out, grasping the stick tighter in her hand.

"Misty? Is that you?"

Blinking in surprise at the familiar voice, Misty lowered her weapon and waited for her visitor to round the corner.

"Chris? What are you doing here?" she asked as Chris Caddel approached. She'd first met Chris several months ago when his grandfather, Joe Caddel, made some furniture for her house. According to Tori, Chris was the one who rescued her the first time Julian Cooper tried to attack her.

"Sorry to pop by unannounced like this," he said,

bending over to let Wally sniff his hand, "but I just heard about Tori and stopped by to see if you could tell me what's been going on?"

Chris was normally very neat and put together, but it looked as if he hadn't slept all night. His thick auburn hair was mussed, and a five o'clock shadow was beginning to form on his handsome face.

Misty nodded in response to his question. "Sure. Why don't you come inside and I'll fix you a cup of coffee?"

Chris agreed, and as Misty fixed the coffee and Wally's breakfast, she asked, "You're just now hearing about the kidnappings?"

"Yes. I've been out of town and didn't get back until late last night." Chris paced around the kitchen as he spoke, his green eyes filled with worry. He'd dated Tori all during high school, and according to Brice, he broke Tori's heart when he ended things between them.

"Here you go," Misty said, handing him a hot cup of coffee.

While Chris sipped the coffee, Misty popped a bagel into the toaster and proceeded to tell him everything that had happened.

"This is awful," he stated in a heavy tone once she was finished. "Tori and I started texting after the attack last week, and I've been wondering why I couldn't get up with her these last few days. Are the police making any progress?"

"Not much, I'm afraid," Misty replied with a sigh.

"Have you spoken to her parents?"

Chris shook his head. "No. I thought her dad was still in the hospital?"

"They let him come home after Tori was kidnapped," Misty explained. "Hey, I know you told the police everything that happened the night Tori was attacked, but is there possibly something you could have missed?"

Chris leaned back in his chair, his expression thoughtful as he pondered Misty's question. After a moment, he said, "The only thing that struck me as odd is Tori said she thought her oven repairman was who attacked her. Julian Cooper is not from around here, though. So, how did he know Tori was all alone out here that night? And when he was at her coffee shop, he was driving a work truck. When I chased him away from here, though, he was in a red Honda Civic."

"You think it wasn't Julian Cooper, then?" Misty asked, studying Chris carefully.

Chris shrugged. "I don't know, Misty," he replied. "All I do know is that when I showed up on the scene, he was familiar enough with his surroundings to run out the back door, jump into his vehicle, and disappear before I could catch him."

"There are so many things about this case that don't make sense," Misty said with a sigh.

Before they could talk more, Misty's phone began to ring, and she saw Adam's name flashing across the screen. Realizing she'd lost track of time and it was a few minutes past nine, she quickly grabbed the phone and answered.

"Hey, I'll be ready in a…"

"Misty, something terrible has happened," Adam interrupted, and Misty could hear the tension in his voice.

"What is it, Adam?" she asked.

"It's Lexi. She was kidnapped this morning. And Misty…there was a message left behind, and it mentions your name."

CHAPTER 22

When Misty arrived at the Dawson home, police cars were everywhere. She saw Adam and Lexi's parents talking to Dylan and Sheriff Ward, and by the looks on their faces, Misty could clearly see they were distraught. Her stomach clenched as she climbed from her car. Was *this* what the note left in her mailbox had meant? Was Lexi's kidnapping her fault?

"Hey Harris," Misty said when she spotted the young rookie. "How did it happen?"

With a heavy sigh, Harris said, "We're not entirely certain yet. All I know is that when Lexi's mom got up this morning, she found a note on the kitchen table from Lexi stating that she'd gone for a run. When Mrs. Dawson stepped outside to get the morning paper, she found Lexi's cellphone and smartwatch lying on the porch. There was an unsent text message on the phone, but I don't know what it said." Nodding toward the sheriff, Harris added, "He said he wanted to see you as soon as you arrived, so you'd better go on over."

Nodding, Misty thanked Harris and walked toward the house. When Dylan spotted her, he motioned for her to join them.

"Mr. and Mrs. Dawson, I'm so sorry about Lexi,"

Misty said, reaching out to the older woman who was crying. When Mrs. Dawson turned away from her with no response and Mr. Dawson simply stood there, glaring at her, Misty swallowed and pulled her hand away.

"Miss Raven, we've just been talking to Adam about what this message could possibly mean," Sheriff Ward stated, his expression tight as he held up Lexi's phone.

Leaning closer, Misty silently read the typed message: *"Misty should have stayed out of it, and so should Lexi's brother. Three have now been taken. Will there be another?"*

"Adam said he went with you yesterday to investigate a few local, abandoned buildings, and Dylan told me about the note you received last night," Sheriff Ward said once she'd finished reading the text message. Raising an eyebrow, he asked in an angry tone, "Just what do you think you're doing, Miss Raven?"

"I was just trying to help," Misty said as hot tears burned the backs of her tired, dry eyes.

Dropping the cell phone into a plastic bag, Sheriff Ward handed the bag over to Dylan, who hadn't spoken a word the entire time.

"Well, it seems that your **help** has caused another woman to be kidnapped, Miss Raven," Sheriff Ward snapped.

Her temper flaring, Misty asked, "I guess I'm also responsible for the kidnapping of the other two women you haven't found yet?"

Clenching his jaw at the implication behind her question, the sheriff stepped closer and pointed his finger in Misty's face. "Stay out of our investigation, Miss Raven," he told her. When she opened her mouth to say something, he added, "That's not a request; it's an order. And if I find out that you haven't obeyed me, I'll have you arrested. You've interfered enough already, and I don't care to have to deal with any more upset and distraught families because of you. Do you understand?"

With a tight nod, Misty looked at Mr. and Mrs. Dawson and said softly, "I'm very sorry," before turning and walking away. She'd just made it back to her car when Adam called her name.

"Misty, wait," he said, grabbing her arm. He forced her to face him, and when she looked up, his black eyes were filled with guilt. "I'm sorry, Misty. I didn't know Sheriff Ward would respond that way when I told him about yesterday."

Pulling her arm away, Misty swiped at her eyes and said, "Apparently, your parents feel the same way he does." Looking at him pointedly, she asked, "Do you?"

In the split second that Adam hesitated, Misty knew the truth. He blamed her for Lexi's kidnapping. If she hadn't been snooping around where she didn't belong, trying to find answers, would Lexi have been taken anyway? Misty didn't know, but she was being blamed for it and felt lower than she had in a very long time.

"No, of course not..."

Misty held up her hand, stopping Adam. With a shake of her head, she said, "I'm sorry. If I'd known this would happen, I never would have interfered. I was just trying to help."

Turning, Misty climbed into her car and drove away. She glanced in the rearview mirror and saw Adam standing there, staring after her. Before she rounded the corner, he turned, and with stooped shoulders, walked back toward his family.

When Misty arrived back home, Patrick Donovan was sitting in front of her house. She parked her car and got out, wondering why he was there.

"Misty, thank God you're alright," he said as he jumped from his car and hurried toward her. "I heard that another woman had been kidnapped, and when I tried to call you and there was no answer, I feared the worst."

"It was Lexi Dawson," she stated in a monotone voice. "And they're blaming me."

His brow furrowing, Patrick asked, "They're blaming you for her kidnapping? Why?"

"I've been doing some investigating of my own, and I guess I got too close to something," she replied with a heavy sigh. She felt completely drained, and like she was carrying the weight of the world on her shoulders. "The kidnapper left a note saying I should have stayed out of it. Sheriff

Ward said if I don't back off, he'll arrest me."

His cheeks flushing, Patrick stood up straighter and declared, "The nerve of him! I never did like that man. I certainly don't plan to vote for him next term."

With a small shrug, Misty said, "Maybe he's right, though. Maybe I **did** endanger those women by poking my nose where it doesn't belong."

"That's not true, Misty," he stated. "I don't believe it for one second. Sheriff Ward is simply acting out because he can't solve the first major crime he's been faced with since he took this job."

Misty wrapped her arms around her waist and swallowed back tears. It seemed all she could do this morning was cry, and she knew she needed to get some rest. How could she possibly lie down, though, and relax with everything that was happening? She appreciated Patrick's words of support, though, and told him so in a choked voice.

Chewing on his lip, Patrick eyed her for a moment before finally asking, "Misty, I know you're going through a lot right now, but can we please talk? It's killing me that I haven't had a chance to explain things."

Too tired to protest, Misty simply nodded and said, "Sure. Come inside and I'll fix us both some coffee."

While Misty fixed the coffee, Mr. Donovan sat at the kitchen table and nervously tapped his fingers on its surface. Misty could see in his eyes how anxious he felt to tell her everything, and she felt a little sorry for him. She'd known the man for almost a year and considered him to be a good friend. The fact that he was her father, though, gave her such an odd feeling. As she joined him at the table with two cups of steaming hot coffee, she wondered how she would feel once he was finished with his story.

Taking a deep breath, Patrick leaned forward and placed his elbows on the table. He took a sip of his coffee, as if hoping to receive some fortification, and then looked up at Misty.

"I'd like to start at the very beginning if that's alright?" he asked. When Misty nodded, he began his story. "I come from a very prominent family in Savannah," he said, glancing down at his coffee cup. "When I was in college, I was coerced by my family to date the daughter of my father's business partner. I didn't want to; we'd always been just friends, but I did it as a way to gain my father's favor. Before I knew it, we were engaged."

Patrick stopped for a moment as he thought back on those days, his face full of misery. "I didn't love her," he continued, "but I didn't know how to get out of it. On the night of our graduation, she and I had a major argument, and I broke it off with her. My father was livid, to say the least, but for once, I didn't care. I'd finally decided to live my own life, and if that meant being disowned by my family, then so be it."

Patrick stood up then and began to walk slowly around the kitchen, his hands pushed deep into his pockets. As if sensing the tension in the air, Wally came to sit next to Misty, bumping her hand with his nose until he'd made room enough to lay his head on her lap.

"With everything that was happening, I needed to get away for a while," Mr. Donovan said. "A distant cousin of mine lived in Dahlonega, so I went to stay with him over the summer. That's when I met your mother." At the mention of Elena, Mr. Donovan's expression softened and a small smile began to pull at his lips. "She was working at the Black Wolf Lodge that summer, which was only about a mile from my cousin's lake house. I was riding down the mountain on a bike one day, which wasn't the smartest idea I'd ever had when I nearly went over the edge to avoid a car that was coming toward me. I over-corrected and crashed into a tree, and the driver of the car jumped out to see if I was okay. That driver was your mother, Misty."

Patrick smiled warmly at Misty as he relived those memories from so long ago. As she listened to him speak, she gently ran her fingers over Wally's soft head, feeling comforted by his presence beside her.

"Elena took me back to the lodge and doctored my cuts and scrapes, and as we began to talk, it seemed that we'd known each other forever. She was shy, and I could tell she didn't open up to people easily, but there was just a connection between us; it was stronger than anything I'd ever felt before." Mr. Donovan sighed, his voice filled with emotion as he said, "She was everything I'd ever dreamed of, Misty. She was beautiful and caring and sensitive, and she understood me in a way that no one else ever had before. We began seeing each other nearly every day after that, only she didn't want me to visit her at the lodge for fear of losing her job. So, we would meet for picnics after she was finished with work or on her days off. We'd drive to Helen and explore the beautiful forest trails and waterfalls. It was like Heaven. I never knew I could love somebody as much as I loved her. That's...that's why I never understood why she left as she did."

His eyes filled with sadness, Patrick reclaimed his seat and said to Misty, "We were going to be married; I'd already proposed and was having a special ring made. I went to see her, to give her the ring, but she was gone. She'd packed her bags and disappeared in the night. I was heartbroken, Misty. I searched for months, but I never found her. When I saw her here in Shady Pines three years later, I thought I was dreaming."

Without saying a word, Misty got up and went into her bedroom to retrieve one of the letters Elena had written to her friend in Dahlonega. When she returned moments later, she handed the letter to Patrick.

"She said you were engaged to someone else," Misty told him as she sat back down.

Patrick read the letter, his face losing its color

when he saw what Elena had written. "Oh, my God," he whispered as realization sunk in. "Avery must have told her that."

Looking up at Misty, he said, "Avery, my ex-fiancé, showed up at my cousin's lake house in an attempt to win me back, but I told her I'd found someone else. When I went into town to pick up the ring, Elena must have stopped by the house to see me." His face filling with sadness, he shook his head and said, "Avery probably told Elena she was my fiancé. Oh, Misty, I'd never even mentioned Avery to her before. She must have thought I was a miserable liar and cheat."

They sat in silence for a moment as the truth sank into both of their battered souls. Mr. Donovan was heartbroken to finally know what had happened between him and Elena, while Misty was still trying to process everything.

"Mr. Donovan," she finally said, breaking the silence, "if you really were engaged to my mother, why didn't you tell me before now? I specifically asked you months ago if you remembered my mother, and you acted as if you barely knew her."

With a sigh, Patrick stood up and began pacing again. "When I told you that I couldn't remember her last name, it was the truth," he said. "I was referring to her married name, though. In order to tell you her maiden name, I would have had to explain all of this to you, and I just didn't feel free to do that."

At the look of confusion on Misty's face, Patrick

sat back down and rubbed his eyes. It wasn't until then that Misty noticed how bloodshot they were. Had he not slept at all the last few days?

"When you first moved to town and asked about your mother, my wife had just died," he said, suddenly looking very tired. "I met Sandra almost two years after I lost your mother. My family and I weren't speaking. I was lonely and depressed, and she was the one who got me back on my feet. She put that spark back into my life, and we'd just gotten married when Elena suddenly showed up in Shady Pines." Shaking his head, Patrick stopped and sat in silence for a moment, staring off into space as he relived those days. Finally, he said, "Seeing her again was like being kicked in the stomach. I didn't tell Sandra, though; she never knew about Elena. She was so good to me, Misty, and I cared about my wife very much. That's why when she died, it felt like I would be smearing her memory somehow by discussing the first woman I loved. The only one I **truly** loved."

Mr. Donovan broke down then and started to cry, and Misty could see the torture and shame on his face. It broke her heart, but she didn't say anything. She didn't know **what** to say.

Pulling a handkerchief from his shirt pocket, Mr. Donovan wiped his eyes and said, "I knew Elena didn't have any family here in the States, so I didn't think telling you her maiden name was necessary. Especially since I knew you'd found Karson." Looking at Misty with blue eyes that swam with guilt and grief, he added, "If you'd told me that Karson Himmel wasn't your real father, though, I would have told you everything, Misty. I promise. It wasn't until Tori told me you'd gone to Dahlonega that I started suspecting something was wrong."

Misty nodded, her fingers absently running through Wally's thick fur around his neck. Her head swam with everything Mr. Donovan had told her. She felt emotional and drained and like she needed to just lie down and cry for a while.

After a few moments of silence, she finally cleared her throat and said, "Thank you for explaining all of this. I know it wasn't easy for you. If…if you don't mind, could I be alone now? I need some time to process all of this."

Mr. Donovan nodded. "Of course. I know it's been a lot, Misty, and I'm so sorry all of this happened. I wish…" his voice became choked then, and he looked down at the floor before continuing. "I wish Elena hadn't left that night so long ago. I wish I'd known about you. How different life would have been for all of us."

Picking up his coat jacket, which he'd draped over one of the barstools, Mr. Donovan turned and walked from the kitchen. Before stepping out of the door, he turned back and said, "I hope you can forgive me, Misty," and then he was gone.

Misty sat in the silent kitchen, not moving and barely breathing. She listened to the sound of Patrick's retreating footsteps, the front door opening and closing, and then his car as he drove away. Finally, after what felt like hours, the tears began to flow, and she leaned her head over on the table and cried. She cried for the life she'd been robbed of, for the mother she barely remembered, and for the heartache Elena's decision to disappear had ultimately caused those most important to her.

CHAPTER 23

Tori

The darkness was beginning to smother her. She felt like she was fading away, slowly, a little bit at a time, and would eventually just blend in with the blackness that surrounded her. He wouldn't leave her with a flashlight for very long; only when he brought her meals, and then he'd take it with him after she'd eaten. Each time, she would gaze at that little light and yearn for the warmth of the sun. Would she ever see it again? Would she ever escape from this black dungeon that felt like it was draining the very life out of her?

She hadn't eaten in hours, and her stomach rumbled angrily. Where was he? Why hadn't he brought her any breakfast? She thought of standing up to pace around the room once again, but her legs were just too weak.

Suddenly, the sound of movement could be heard out in the hall. Tilting her head, Tori listened intently. Footsteps, grunting, and then a scream echoed off the walls. Jumping up, her blood pumping, Tori raced across the room and pressed her ear against the door. Someone was struggling; that was plain enough. But who?

"You won't get away with this!" someone screeched, and Tori could have sworn the voice belonged to Lexi Dawson.

Just then, the sound of a hand connecting forcefully with skin echoed down the hallway, and Tori flinched. The struggling and screaming stopped, and Tori heard the door across from hers open. A *thud* met her ears, the door slammed, and then it was locked.

As the sound of his footsteps faded away, Tori fought back the feeling of panic that continued to grow worse and worse. He'd kidnapped again, and she knew he didn't simply plan to keep them here forever. No, he had a much bigger, darker plan, and Tori knew if they weren't found soon, they didn't have much longer left to live.

Misty

It was mid-afternoon when a frantic knock suddenly sounded on Misty's front door. With a sigh, she walked through the house to open it, catching a glimpse of herself in the foyer mirror along the way. She looked a fright; her eyes were red and swollen from crying so much, she was pale as a ghost, and her hair hadn't been washed in days. She was completely wiped out and felt like she barely had enough strength to put one foot in front of the other.

"Misty, where on earth have you been?" Brice

asked as soon as she opened the door. "I've been trying to get up with you for hours."

Her head pounding, Misty held up a hand to shade her eyes from the sun. "Sorry, I guess my phone must be on vibrate," she mumbled.

Frowning, Brice asked, "What's wrong? Are you okay?"

Misty sighed. "I'm better than Tori, Anna, and Lexi."

"You heard about Lexi, huh?" Brice asked. "That's why I've been trying to call you."

"Adam told me right after it happened," she replied. "I guess you've heard that I'm to blame?"

His forehead wrinkling, Brice said, "No. What are you talking about?"

Motioning for him to come inside, Misty said, "I have a raging headache, and the sunlight is killing me. Come inside and I'll explain."

They went into the living room and sat on the sofa. Rubbing her temples, Misty crossed her legs and told Brice what happened. When she'd finished, her head felt even worse.

"It's ridiculous for anyone to say this is your fault," Brice stated. "Sheriff Ward is just blaming anyone he can because his department can't find any leads. You heard what Harris said the other day; the sheriff has been on Dylan's back, too. This is not your fault, Misty."

Misty stood up and shrugged. "I don't know, Brice. Maybe he's right. If Adam and I hadn't been snooping around, maybe his sister would still be at home with her parents."

As Misty spoke, she walked over to the window that looked out into her backyard. Brice didn't say anything for a moment, and Misty wondered if he secretly blamed her, too. As she stared out the window, she noticed the pine trees were swaying and the sky was turning dark in that direction. A storm was on the way, it seemed.

"You and Adam were together all day yesterday?"

When Brice chose that question to ask, Misty turned to look at him in surprise. He was staring at her, his face solemn, and Misty wondered what was going on behind those blue eyes of his.

"Yes," she replied, tucking a strand of hair behind one ear. "He figured out what I was up to and followed me. After that, he went with me because he said it was too dangerous."

"He wasn't wrong about that," Brice stated. Clearing his throat, he asked, "So, you've decided to date him after all?"

Her nerves were on edge, and for some reason, Misty felt very irritated by that question. "No, Brice," she snapped. "We were out looking for Tori and Anna; I wouldn't exactly call that a date."

His jaw clenching at her tone, Brice stood up and said, "When are you going to make up your mind about him, Misty? You can't just keep stringing him along."

Misty's mouth dropped open. *Stringing* him along? How had the conversation made such a wild and unexpected turn? And why was Brice attacking her this way? After the day she'd had, she felt hurt and angry and like she wanted to throw something at Brice's head.

"Why exactly do you think it's any of *your* business?" she asked, raising an eyebrow.

His eyes flashing, Brice stepped closer and wrapped his fingers around her arm. "After that kiss we shared in Dahlonega, I'd say it's my business," he ground out.

"Oh, you mean the kiss we shared after you told me you weren't interested in having another relationship?" she demanded.

Misty could hear Wally pacing around in the kitchen, and she knew he was wondering what was going on. She didn't exactly know herself, but her blood was boiling with irritation, her head still pounded, and her skin sizzled at Brice's touch.

"I said that months ago," Brice shot back.

Raising yet another eyebrow, Misty asked in a sarcastic tone, "Oh, so I guess that means you no longer feel that way?"

"That's exactly what it means."

Misty blinked, totally caught off guard by that response. What was Brice saying? That he now wanted to date her? Her head was spinning and she couldn't seem to make sense of her thoughts; she couldn't even remember how this conversation got started in the first place.

"So, what are you saying?" she asked, the question coming out as more of a croak.

A rumble of thunder suddenly shook the house, startling them both, and Brice blew out a heavy breath.

"You just need to figure out what you want," he stated as he released her arm and took a step back. "That's all I'm saying."

As Brice turned and walked away, Misty stared at his retreating figure in disbelief. Had he really just flipped everything back on her? She couldn't believe it, nor was she going to let him get away with it.

Stomping through the house after him, Misty caught up with him in the foyer. The lights were off and she could see flashes of lightning coming from outside, but nothing could match the storm in her spirit.

"How dare you say that *I* need to figure out what *I* want?" she all but yelled at him. When he spun around to face her, she rammed a finger into his chest, her eyes flashing with indignation. "**You** are the one who told me you weren't interested in another relationship, then you kissed me on a mountaintop, and then you acted sorry you did it afterward. If anyone is stringing anyone along, Brice Barlow, it's **you**. How can you say I need to figure out what I want when you haven't told me what **you** want? You've done nothing but..."

"You want to know what I want?" he interrupted, his blue gaze intense as he stared down at her through the shadows. "Fine. I want **you**, Misty."

Misty's heart caught as Brice grabbed her by the arms and pulled her closer. He dipped his head and covered her mouth with his, stealing the very breath from her lungs. He slowly moved them forward until her back was pressed against the foyer wall, and Misty felt her hands move up his chest and wind tightly around his neck.

Their kiss on the mountaintop was sudden and unexpected, like this one. But there was a passion and fervency this time that made Misty's head spin. He wrapped his arms firmly around her waist, pulling her closer against him. She could feel the warmth radiating off his body as his heart pounded against her own, and all she could think and feel in this moment was him. She had always been alone and done things her own way, but the last few days had shown her that she needed someone, and feeling the strength in Brice's arms as he held her tightly made her feel safe and protected. It also made her heart race out of control, which frightened her a bit, and when he pulled away moments later, she felt breathless and lightheaded.

"I didn't regret the kiss in Dahlonega," he said, his breath warm against her face. "And I don't regret this one."

Brice stepped back, breaking all contact between them, and Misty stared at him in silence, unable to speak. His beautiful eyes were filled with warmth and passion, and the way he looked at her made her weak in the knees.

"When you decide what you want, Misty, I'll be waiting."

With those words, Brice turned and walked out into the rain. Misty went to the door and watched him leave, her heart soaring and feeling conflicted all at the same time. With the rain beating on the porch roof and wind whipping through the trees, Misty watched as Brice drove away.

CHAPTER 24

The rain continued all day Friday and on into Saturday. By the time it stopped, it was early afternoon, and Misty had done more work on the house than she had in weeks. She was on her way downstairs to fix herself some lunch when her phone rang.

"Misty, it's Dylan. Can you come down to the station? I'd like to run something by you."

Wondering what was going on, Misty agreed and quickly changed her clothes. As she pulled into the police station parking lot twenty minutes later, she hoped she wouldn't see Sheriff Ward. All she needed was another scolding.

"Hey, thanks for coming by," Dylan said when she stepped into his office. He had a map lying on his desk with some markings, and he motioned for her to step closer and take a look. Pointing to a few of the locations he had marked, he asked, "Are these the places you and Adam visited Thursday?"

Looking over the map carefully, Misty nodded, wondering why he hadn't just asked Adam. When he saw the question in her eyes, Dylan said, "Adam got called away on a job last night. He should be back in the morning, but I wanted to verify this was all correct as soon as possible."

"It's all correct," Misty said. "Are you going to

check these places out again?"

Looking up at her from his desk chair, Dylan lowered his voice and said, "Apparently, you and Adam were getting close to something, or else the kidnapper wouldn't have reacted the way he did. I'm going out to these places personally today to check out the surrounding areas."

"Will you let me know if you find anything?" Misty asked.

Dylan nodded. "Yes. And Misty, I'm sorry Sheriff Ward spoke to you that way yesterday. It was uncalled for."

Misty was shocked that Dylan was taking her side but felt relieved that he apparently didn't blame her.

"Thank you, Dylan," she said with a smile. "Good luck today."

As she left his office, Misty felt a heaviness settle on her shoulders. Today was Saturday; they were running out of time. What would happen to Tori and the other two women if they weren't found by Monday?

"Hello, Miss Raven."

Misty was so lost in her thoughts that she hadn't noticed Samuel, Kyra Kirby's boyfriend, walking toward her.

"Hi, Samuel," she said, shaking his outstretched hand. "How are you?"

Glancing around, as if to make certain no one was listening, Samuel stepped closer and said, "Be careful, Miss Raven. Something isn't right about these kidnappings."

Her brow furrowing, Misty asked, "What do you mean?"

"In all my years working at the police force in Charleston, I've learned a few things," he said. "I just wanted to warn you to be extra careful."

Sheriff Ward's voice could be heard coming from around the corner, and Samuel quickly walked away. As Misty headed outside to her car, she couldn't get Samuel's words out of her mind. Was he really just trying to warn her, or was he threatening her in some way?

After leaving the police station, Misty stopped at the small pizzeria in town to grab a late lunch. When she stepped inside, she spotted Noah Welch standing in line, waiting to order. Thinking of her conversation with Adam about how Noah hardly had any friends, Misty stepped up behind him and tapped him lightly on the shoulder.

"Hi, Noah," she said with a friendly smile.

Turning in surprise, Noah said, "Oh, uh, hello."

"Do you come here often?" Misty asked in an attempt to make friendly conversation.

Noah shook his head. "No, not really. I normally eat at home."

Noah turned back around then to place his order, and Misty noticed the tip of a Band-Aid poking out from beneath his collar. She wondered how he would have gotten a scratch or cut in such an odd area, but assumed that's why he bought those first-aid supplies in Cloud Haven.

After he'd placed his order, Noah nodded to Misty and walked away to claim a table. As he moved slowly across the room, she noticed he was limping slightly.

"Can I help you?"

The cashier cleared her throat then, and Misty jerked her attention away from Noah. With a smile, she ordered a personal pan pizza with a side of ranch dressing and an order of cheesy bread. After paying for the meal, Misty walked over to Noah's table.

"Mind if I join you?" she asked.

Noah's face flushed at the request, but he nodded and motioned to the seat across from him.

"I guess you've heard about Lexi Dawson?" Misty asked after she'd taken her seat.

"Yes, I did," he replied. "It's terrible."

"You grew up with her, too, right?" Misty asked.

"I did," he replied, glancing down at his glass of tea. "She and I always ran in different circles, though, so I was never a close friend or anything."

"You and Tori are friends, though," she stated with a smile. "You go by her coffee shop pretty often, don't you?"

"Oh, well, Tori has always been very nice to me," he said warmly. "She was different from Lexi and the other girls at school; she actually noticed me and went out of her way to be nice to me."

Taking a sip of her own tea, Misty said, "That's Tori for you. She really is the best." When Noah nodded but didn't respond, she added, "I know how it is to not fit in at school. I was always the weird foster kid who didn't have any parents, so I heard plenty of unkind remarks in my day."

Noah looked at her in surprise and asked, "Really? I would never have thought of you as being weird, Miss Raven. You're like Tori; very kind and thoughtful."

Misty wondered how he could say that about her when she hadn't even remembered meeting him in the first place, but their food arrived at the table just then and she was immediately distracted. As Noah dove into the extra cheesy pizza he'd ordered, she wondered how his "sensitive stomach" would handle this meal.

"It's nice of you to eat with me, Miss Raven," Noah said after a moment of silence. "I've wanted to get to know you better, but I didn't think you'd care to be friends with someone like me."

Misty raised her eyebrows and asked, "What do you mean, someone like you?"

Noah shrugged and looked away. "Oh, you know," he replied shyly. "I've never really had a lot of friends."

"Neither have I," she told him. "And please, call me Misty."

As they ate the delicious meal, the awkward tension between them began to ease a bit. Misty wondered what Lexi Dawson had done to Noah in school that made him dislike her so much, but she didn't voice the question. Perhaps Lexi was just a different person back then; people often change as they grow older. Since Noah apparently wasn't a fan of Lexi's, though, why had he asked Adam about her when they'd seen him in Cloud Haven? He'd acted then as if he and Lexi were friends. Maybe he was just trying to be nice.

By the time Misty's plate was clean, Noah had told her all about his cat, Tiger, and how he'd managed to fix his kitchen sink by watching DIY videos online.

"So, Noah, do you have any hobbies?" Misty asked, interrupting him as he began to veer off into yet another conversation about Tiger and how the cat had been suffering from diarrhea lately.

Noah thought the question over for a moment. "I enjoy writing," he finally said.

"Oh? What type of writing?" she wanted to know.

"I like to write poems," he replied. He then blushed and looked away as he quickly added, "But I'm not very good."

"I'm sure you're quite good at it," she told him with a smile. Grabbing her purse, she said, "Well, I'd better be heading home now. It was nice talking to you, Noah. Thanks for letting me join you."

Standing up, he said eagerly, "Anytime."

As Misty got into her car and drove away, she wished she'd asked Noah to let her read a few of his poems sometime; she imagined they really were quite good.

Once Misty was back home, she could barely concentrate on her work for the rest of the day. It was killing her not being able to do anything to help find the three missing women. She was afraid, though, that if she continued her search of the old buildings left on her list, Sheriff Ward would make good on his promise and arrest her.

Just before going to bed that night, she realized Dylan had never come by to retrieve the last note she'd received in her mailbox, and she'd forgotten to take it with her when she went to the station. She grabbed her phone and texted him a reminder, and then she asked how his search had gone. He never answered, and she finally drifted off into a much-needed deep sleep.

CHAPTER 25

The next morning, as Misty got ready for church, all she could think about was Tori. They had one more day. Just one. Was Tori even still alive? Was it foolish to think that, after almost a week, they'd be able to rescue her?

When Misty walked into the church, she spotted Brice, and her heart immediately caught in her chest. She hadn't spoken to him at all yesterday, and when he turned and looked directly at her, she almost tripped and fell flat on her face.

"Misty, how are you holding up?"

Turning to look at Penny in surprise, Misty said, "Oh, hi, Penny. I thought you were out of town?"

Giving Misty a quick hug, Penny said, "I got back last night. My cousin got sick, so we all came home early."

Theo stood next to Penny and didn't look very thrilled at her coming back so soon. He stared at Misty, not saying a word. With a raised eyebrow, she stated, "Hello, Theo. I ran into your friend Blaze the other day. He said he'd like his money back."

Theo's eyes widened at Misty's words, and he glanced quickly at Penny before saying, "I don't know anyone by that name."

He then took Penny by the arm and began pulling her away. She glanced between him and Misty with a look of confusion, and Misty read her lips as she asked him what was going on. He shook his head and said it was nothing, but both he and Misty knew better than that. What exactly he was up to, though, Misty couldn't say, but she had her suspicions about him.

The service was just beginning to start when Misty joined the Barlows on their pew. Poor Mr. Neil sat in a wheelchair, his face ashen, and Mrs. Amy had thick, black circles lining her eyes. Misty sat between her and Pops, with Brice on the other side. All during the service, Misty could feel Brice's presence as if it sizzled. He looked over at her a few times, and when their eyes met, her heart caught. She saw Adam's parents sitting across from them, and when the pastor requested prayer for the three missing women, Mrs. Dawson covered her face with a handkerchief and leaned against her husband.

The sermon that Pastor Alvin preached was about peace, and all Misty wanted to do was cry as she listened. She needed peace right now and the strength that came with it, but every time she looked over at Anna's and Lexi's families or heard Mrs. Amy sniffle next to her, she felt the tension and anxiety start to creep back in. She'd solved many mysteries over the years and had been faced with dangerous situations before, but never had she experienced anything quite like this. Tori was her very best friend, and it was killing Misty to think that she might lose her.

By the time the service was over, Misty's nerves were shot. She hugged Mrs. Amy goodbye and then hurried out early. She just couldn't deal any longer with the sympathetic looks everyone kept giving the families of the missing women. Plus, seeing the Dawsons brought that ugly episode back to her mind, as well as the conversation she'd had later with Brice. When she finally made it to her car, her head was pounding all over again.

"I'm telling you, Adrian, I *know* what we saw."

The whispered voices caught Misty's attention, and she turned to find three young boys standing near her car.

"Well, I've never seen a ghost there before," Adrian stated.

"But *you're* the one who told us the place was haunted!" the third boy cried.

All three boys suddenly realized they had an audience and turned to find Misty watching them. Adrian and one of the boys took off like they'd been caught committing a crime, while the third boy smiled innocently at Misty and said, "Good morning, Miss Raven."

Smiling in return, Misty stepped closer and said, "Good morning. Your name is Mason, right?"

Mason nodded. "Yes, ma'am."

"If you don't mind my asking, Mason, what were you and your friends talking about?" Misty asked curiously.

Mason glanced nervously around as if looking for a way of escape. Stuffing his hands into his pockets, he shuffled his feet for a moment and muttered, "Oh, nothin' really. Me and Lucas just thought we saw a ghost, that's all."

Raising her eyebrows, Misty asked, "Really? Where was this?" When Mason began to look like he was going to make a run for it, she quickly added, "My house was supposedly haunted when I bought it, you know, so I love ghosts. Your secret is safe with me, I promise."

Mason eyed her for a moment, his lower lip pulled between his teeth. Finally, he stepped closer and said in a low voice, "You know where the old asylum is?"

Misty frowned, not sure she'd ever heard of the place. "I don't think so," she replied.

"It's on the other side of the woods, near Lucas's place," he said. "We went there last night and saw a ghost looking down at us from one of the windows."

"What did this ghost look like?" Misty asked.

"Scary," he replied, his eyes wide. "White hair, pale skin, and big eyes. She had her mouth open like she was screaming or something. It was creepy."

Before Misty could ask him any more questions, Mason's parents called to him and he took off. People were beginning to stream out of the church, so Misty took off as well before anyone could catch her. As she drove home, her thoughts were filled with what Mason had told her. How had she never heard of this supposed asylum? And what had the boys *really* seen in that window?

Misty didn't know where Lucas lived, but as soon as she got home, she grabbed her computer and began doing some research. It didn't take her long to find an article written about the Shady Pines Asylum. It was built in the late 1800s and stayed open until the 1970s. When Misty noticed where the now-empty building was located, her eyes widened. It was located deep in the woods, only a couple of miles from where the Dawsons lived.

Closing her computer, Misty stood up and began to pace around the room. Dare she go check it out? Or perhaps she should just tell Dylan. What if it was simply another dead end, though? Sheriff Ward would have her hide if she sent Dylan on a wild goose chase when they only had one day left.

After a few moments of pondering it all over, Misty made up her mind. She'd go there herself tonight when no one would be able to see her approaching. And if Sheriff Ward found out and arrested her, then so be it. Her best friend's life was at stake, and it wasn't time for Misty to back down now.

CHAPTER 26

Tori

He'd left the flashlight this time. When he took her tray of food, he'd seemed distracted, and Tori nearly shouted for joy when he walked out without taking the light with him. Now she could continue working on digging that nail out of the baseboard.

Hurrying across the room where her blanket lay against the wall, Tori dropped to her knees and shoved the blanket aside. Somehow during the night, she'd found a nail slightly protruding from one of the baseboards, and she'd tried working it out, but it was too dark to see what she was doing. As she shined the light on the wall now, she saw that the nail was bent inward, but with a little work, she felt that she could pull it out. Then perhaps she could use it to pick the lock on her door.

Tori dug at that nail for what felt like hours. Her fingers were blistered and starting to bleed, but she didn't quit. She had to get out of this place. She **had** to. Finally, the nail turned, and after one last jerk, it slid from its hole. Tori immediately jumped to her feet and ran over to the door, where she kneeled down and began wiggling the sharp point inside the keyhole. As she worked, she hoped he wouldn't hear her. If he caught her, he'd kill her. She knew it.

Sweat dripped down Tori's brow. Her fingers trembled as anxiety made her heart pound. The nail twisted and turned, but nothing happened. Frustration nipped at her heels, but Tori kept trying. She couldn't give up.

Suddenly, the lock clicked, and Tori caught her breath. The door was unlocked! Picking up the flashlight, she slowly eased the door open and peered out into the hall. A single light flickered in the long corridor, but no sound or movement could be seen or heard. Tori's legs trembled as she stepped through the door and out into the hallway, her eyes searching every shadowy corner. It seemed he wasn't around. For now.

Tori knew she should escape while she had the chance, but she couldn't leave Anna and Lexi behind. Still holding the nail in her hand, she hurried across the hall and began finagling with the doorknob.

"Who's there?"

The frightened voice called out from the other side of the door, and Tori whispered, "It's okay, Lexi. I'm trying to get you out."

"Tori? You're free? Run while you can!"

Ignoring her friend's demand, Tori kept trying to get the stubborn lock to turn. She was so focused on the job at hand that she didn't hear the approaching footsteps. When the door at the end of the hall opened, she gasped and swung the flashlight in that direction. As the beam landed on a familiar face, Tori's mouth dropped open.

"Hayden?"

Misty

It was almost nine o'clock when Misty made her way out to the old asylum. The night was dark, and as her car bumped down the rutted dirt road, she hoped she wasn't making a mistake.

She was almost there; she could see the break in the woods up ahead where the entrance to the asylum property began. Stopping the car, Misty grabbed her backpack and stepped out into the eerily quiet night. The woods were thick and dark, and no sound could be heard over the crunching of Misty's footsteps. When she reached the opening in the trees, she stopped and stared at the old structure that rested in the midst of tall grass and weeds. She didn't see anyone, but there seemed to be something about the building that said it wasn't empty.

Holding tightly to her flashlight, Misty crept closer to the old asylum. The building was in horrible disrepair, but she immediately noticed that none of the windows on the second floor were broken. She also spotted that the front door had recently been replaced.

Carefully, Misty grasped hold of the doorknob,

opened the front door, and stepped inside. The front room looked like it had once been a receiving area, but dirt and trash lay all over the floor. Dusty chairs that were covered in cobwebs sat around like old relics ready to testify of the people who had once rested their weary bodies there. An old telephone sat on the front desk, its cord still plugged into a phone jack in the wall, and a filing cabinet stood half open against the wall. One thing that Misty didn't miss was the visible footprints that tracked through the dusty floor. Someone had been here recently.

Misty quietly made her way through the large, open room and into a long hallway. On either side were doors that led into what appeared to have once been exam rooms. In one such room, Misty saw a sleeping mat spread out on the floor, along with a large cooler. Dirty cups and plates rested on a table, and a large bag of trash sat in the corner. Was someone living out here?

Suddenly, the thumping of footsteps sounded overhead, and Misty's heart jumped. Grabbing her cell phone, she hurriedly dialed Dylan, but he didn't answer. She left a quick message on his voicemail, telling him where she was and what was going on, and then hung up. Should she wait for him to call her back? No, she needed to know who was upstairs.

Shoving her phone back into her pocket, Misty grabbed her Taser gun and made her way to the staircase at the end of the hall. As she carefully and quietly went up the stairs, she began to hear voices. When she recognized one of them as belonging to Tori, her steps quickened.

"Hayden, what are *you* doing here?" she heard Tori ask.

Misty stopped for a moment, blinking in surprise. Hayden Brownley was here?

"You should have run while you had the chance, Miss Barlow," was Hayden's response, and Misty immediately recognized his voice.

"You…you mean you're the one who kidnapped me?" Tori gasped. "I thought Julian Cooper was the one responsible."

Hayden laughed. "He was, sort of. You see, Julian is my half-brother and we've been doing this sort of thing for years."

"D-doing what sort of thing?" Tori wanted to know.

"We travel around from city to city, picking out young, attractive women who live by themselves," he replied in a casual tone. "When we stopped in Shady Pines and spotted you a few months ago, we decided you were our next victim. Luckily, the house next to yours was for sale."

"So, you've been stalking me and planning this whole thing for months?" Tori gasped.

"Oh, the planning is half the fun," Hayden replied with a laugh. "I sneaked into your shop that Friday night and made certain you would need a repairman for your oven. I knew you wouldn't be able to find anyone on the weekend, so the plan was pretty much foolproof. If it hadn't worked, though, we would have thought of something else."

"So, Julian came to my coffee shop, but *you* were the one who attacked me at Misty's house?"

"That's right. I waited until he left your shop and then I followed you. I know how to imitate his voice, just in case you managed to get away from me. When you did and said you thought it was Julian instead of me who attacked you, boy was I relieved."

Misty couldn't believe her ears. Clutching the Taser gun, she began to ease her way further up the stairs.

"What...what do you plan to do with us?" Tori asked, fear in her voice.

"That's all according to how..."

The step beneath Misty's foot suddenly let out a loud creak, and then Hayden stopped talking. Flinching, Misty silently waited, wondering if he would discover where she was hiding. When the pounding of his footsteps suddenly sounded as he ran toward the staircase, Misty jerked back against the wall and waited. Her heart pounding, she held the Taser gun tightly in her hand and prayed he wouldn't kill her before she could use the weapon.

The door to the stairway flung open, and Misty pressed herself even further into the corner. She shined her flashlight into Hayden's face, the look in his eyes chilling as he lunged toward her. With a yelp of fear, she aimed her Taser gun at his throat and pressed the button. Hayden jerked back as the electric currents connected with his skin, and Misty stared in horror as he stumbled backward and tumbled down the stairs. He landed at the bottom of the second level with a *thud,* and then just lay there, unmoving.

CHAPTER 27

Misty stood there, stunned. Her heart was pounding so fiercely that she feared she might faint. The whole thing happened so fast that she'd barely had time to think, and now she wondered if she'd just killed a man.

"Misty? Are you okay?"

Two cold and trembling hands grabbed her by the arm, and Misty turned to look into her best friend's wide, frightened eyes.

"Oh, Tori," Misty cried, pulling her friend into a tight hug. "Thank God you're okay."

They stood there for a moment, crying, until Tori finally pulled back and said, "We have to go get Anna and Lexi." Glancing down the stairs, she asked hesitantly, "Do...do you think he has the keys?"

Misty looked down at Hayden and swallowed past the lump in her throat. "I'll go check," she said in a shaky voice.

On trembling legs, Misty walked back down the stairs, drawing closer and closer to the body that lay so still and quiet. What if he was awake and just pretending to be unconscious? What if, when she reached his side, he grabbed her and pushed her down the remaining set of stairs?

Misty reached his side and took a deep breath,

trying to remain calm. If he wasn't dead and simply unconscious, she needed to hurry before he woke up. Kneeling down, she began to feel around his pockets, relief flooding over her when her fingers landed on a set of keys.

Pulling them from his pocket, Misty had just stood back up when Hayden moaned and began to stir. Her heart jumping, she hurried back upstairs and into the hallway where Tori waited before one of the closed doors.

"Lexi is in this one," Tori said.

Misty hurriedly began trying each key, a sense of urgency making her fingers shake so badly she almost dropped the keys several times. Finally, one of the keys slid into place and the lock turned. Lexi pushed the door open and threw her arms around both women.

"Thank God," she gasped.

The three women then hurried to Anna's room, and it thankfully didn't take as long to find the right key that time. They'd just opened the door to Anna's room when the sound of footsteps could be heard on the staircase.

"Anna?" Misty called out when the girl didn't immediately emerge from the room.

Shining her flashlight into the dark room, Misty spotted Anna lying on the floor, motionless.

"Is she dead?" Tori gasped.

Hurrying inside the room after Lexi, Misty kneeled beside Anna as Lexi felt for a pulse. They could hear the footsteps drawing closer, and Misty knew they didn't have much longer.

"Is she alive?" Misty whispered, reaching for her Taser once again.

Lexi nodded. "Yes. I think she's been drugged."

"He's coming!" Tori cried from the doorway.

Her heart kicking into overdrive, Misty told the other two women to grab Anna while she ran into the hallway, ready to defend herself again. She could see a shadow making its way to the top of the staircase, and she hurried that way to press her back against the wall beside the doorway.

A large hand slowly crept past the doorframe, and Misty's eyes widened when she realized the hand was holding a gun. Taking a deep breath, she steeled herself in readiness to strike, hoping this wouldn't be the end for all of them.

"Misty? Are you up here?"

Blinking, Misty relaxed at the familiar voice, but then tensed again when she remembered Hayden had said he could imitate other voices.

"Dylan? Is that you?" she asked uncertainly.

Dylan's face peered around the corner at her, and Misty almost fainted with relief.

"Thank God," she breathed. Pointing down the stairs, she asked, "Did you see...?"

Dylan nodded. "Yes, I saw Hayden. He's dead, Misty. You can tell me all about it later at the station. Right now, I need to call for backup and get you all out of here."

The events that followed all happened in a blur of flashing police lights, dozens of questions, and tears of relief. Tori and Lexi were taken to the clinic in town to be checked out, while Anna was rushed to the hospital in Savannah. Sheriff Ward asked Misty to come to the station so he could take down her statement, and as she sat in his cold, barren office later that night, she suddenly felt very lonely. After watching how Tori's and Lexi's families showered them with hugs and smiles of joy when they were notified about their daughters, Misty realized once again how much she'd missed.

"Tell me again what you heard and how Hayden Brownley was killed," Sheriff Ward said, pen in hand.

Misty flinched at that last word. Killed. She'd killed a man. In all the years she'd lived, she never expected to be responsible for the loss of someone else's life. What she didn't understand, though, was why he'd seemed to be waking up when she was grabbing the keys from his pocket. Had he simply been taking his last breath before he died from his injuries?

Wrapping her arms around herself, Misty settled into the hard office chair and once again told Sheriff Ward everything that had happened. As she spoke, she realized how exhausted she was. It had been a long week; probably the longest she'd ever lived, but Misty was beyond thankful that her friend was safe and no longer in any danger.

Once she was finished, Sheriff Ward set down his pen and sighed. After a moment, he looked at her and said, "I'm in a bit of a bind here, Miss Raven. A man was killed tonight because you took it upon yourself to once again interfere in a police investigation. I should really press charges against you for this, especially since I told you to stay out of it."

Misty sat there in stunned silence. Once she was able to get her mind around what he'd just said, she leaned forward in her chair and stated, "If not for me, Sheriff, those women would still be at the hands of a maniac who quite possibly planned to kill them all tomorrow. I considered telling you what the boy said about seeing a "ghost" at the asylum, but I knew you would have simply reprimanded me and told me to mind my own business. When I got there tonight and realized the building wasn't empty, I called Officer Mitchell, but he didn't answer. I did what I felt I had to do to save my friends, which is more than I can say for *you* and your department."

Sheriff Ward's face turned more and more red as she spoke, and at those last words, he slammed his hand down on his desk and opened his mouth. Before he could speak, however, Misty stood up and said, "Do what you must, Sheriff, but know that I'll live the rest of my life with the guilt of knowing I was responsible for the death of another human being. If you *do* press charges, then you should also know that I'll have plenty to say at my hearing regarding how you and your department failed to rescue those women and how it took an amateur citizen to save them."

Misty spun on her heel and marched out of his office, her heart pounding but head held high. She was tired of being talked down to, of being treated like a second-rate citizen. She'd never had anyone to stand up for her and fight her battles, so she'd had to learn at a very young age how to stand up for herself. It wasn't very often, though, that she would speak to someone the way she'd just spoken to Sheriff Ward, but she was tired and drained and emotionally exhausted. If only she could get out of this place and get home, she planned to have a good, long cry.

"Are you alright, Miss Raven?"

Turning, Misty saw Samuel standing behind the front desk. She wondered why he was working so late, but then assumed it had to do with everything that had happened.

"Yes, I'm fine," she replied, forcing a smile. "Thank you for asking."

"What you did tonight took a lot of courage," he said, his eyes filled with admiration as he took a step closer to Misty. "I'm just happy you're all okay."

"So am I, Samuel," she replied.

He was drawing closer to her as if he had more to say, but Misty was too tired to keep talking. With a small wave, she turned and hurried out the door.

As she drove home, hot tears blurred her

vision and slipped silently down her cheeks. Even though Hayden was a crazed lunatic, the fact that she'd killed someone still weighed heavily on her shoulders. And what would she do if Sheriff Ward really pressed charges? Would the whole town agree with him, or would they support her? She knew at least some of them would support her, like the Barlows, but she still felt very burdened and overwhelmed. And very much alone.

CHAPTER 28

A couple of days went by, and it seemed that Julian Cooper had disappeared for good. The Shady Pines police, as well as the police department in Savannah, made an all-out attempt to locate him, but he was nowhere to be found. Sheriff Ward told the local citizens that he didn't expect Cooper to come back to the area, so the town finally started to relax.

Anna Douglas was back home from the hospital. She was severely dehydrated and suffering from the effects of the drugs in her system, but it seemed that she was going to be okay. Lexi had gone back to her home in Atlanta, and Tori was staying with her parents for a few days. Misty had stopped by to see Tori on Monday and was struck by how pale her friend looked. Tori hadn't talked much about what happened, and Misty understood that she needed time. It was killing Misty not to run to her friend, though, and tell her everything that had happened with Patrick Donovan. Once Tori was feeling better, she intended to pour her heart out to her friend.

It was late Wednesday afternoon, and Misty was upstairs working in one of the guest bedrooms when she heard Tori's voice downstairs.

"Is anybody home?" Tori called out.

"I'm upstairs," Misty called in return.

Minutes later, Tori stuck her head into the bedroom. "Hey," she said with a smile. "Wow, this room is looking great."

Putting down her screwdriver, Misty went over and gave her friend a hug. Tori looked much more rested and seemed more relaxed than when Misty last saw her.

"Thanks," she replied, pulling back to look at Tori. "How are you doing?"

With a sigh, Tori sat down on a nearby stool and said, "I'm doing better, but it's not easy to get over something like this. Thank God I wasn't hurt, though. Things could have been so much worse. I'll just be glad when the nightmares stop."

Misty sat on the windowsill and looked over at her friend. "Give yourself time," she said. "It's natural to feel this way after such a traumatic event. You'll get back to normal soon, though. I promise."

"I hope so," she replied with a small smile.

"Did you know it was Hayden the whole time?" Misty asked, hoping her friend wouldn't mind talking about it.

Tori shook her head. "No," she replied. "He either wore a mask when he came into my room or shone a light in my eyes so I couldn't see him. I was shocked when I broke out of my room and saw him in that hallway."

"You didn't recognize his voice?" Misty asked, tilting her head curiously.

"He always spoke in an odd, hoarse tone," Tori replied with a slight shiver. "I guess it wasn't always Hayden that came into my room, though. I suppose he and Julian traded places."

If their normal routine was to kidnap women, have their way with them, and then kill them, why hadn't they done so in this case? Why had they waited a whole week and kidnapped two other women? The whole thing still didn't make sense to Misty, but she didn't voice her questions to Tori. She figured they might never know all the answers, and bringing everything up again to her friend was pointless.

"One of them did try to attack me once," Tori stated in a soft voice as tears filled her eyes. "I escaped, but he caught me. After he dragged me back to that horribly lonely, dark room, he said he'd make you pay for what I'd done. I was terrified, Misty."

"Someone *did* try to kidnap me, you know," Misty said. "He tranquilized poor Wally and threw me into the trunk of his car. Some stranger saved my life, though. I guess I'll never know who that was."

Tori sighed and shook her head. "Well, at least it's all over now. I'm so glad you're okay; I was scared out of my mind that he'd do something to hurt you." Glancing down at her watch, she said, "Wow, I didn't realize how late it was. I haven't had a thing to eat since breakfast. I think I'll go downstairs and fix myself a sandwich. Do you want anything?"

"Just a glass of tea," Misty replied. "I'm almost finished up here, and then I'll join you in the kitchen. There's a lot I need to tell you."

As Tori went downstairs, Misty grabbed her screwdriver and climbed up on a stepladder to finish replacing the light fixture. It took longer than she'd expected, and when Misty jumped off the stepladder and wiped off her hands, she realized nearly twenty minutes had passed. She took off her work apron and was just about to head downstairs when a loud creak sounded out in the hallway.

"Did you give up waiting for me and decide to just bring your sandwich up here?" Misty called out.

When Tori didn't answer, Misty looked over at the bedroom door, which was cracked open a few inches. The light out in the hallway was turned off, so all she could see was darkness. She stood in silence for a moment, listening, but all she could hear was the faint whir of the air conditioner. Was Tori eating by herself in the kitchen? Perhaps the creak she'd heard was simply the sound of her old house settling.

She was reaching out for her phone when she heard it again. This time, however, the creak was louder and much closer.

"Tori?" she called again. "Is that you?"

There was no response, and Misty felt her whole body begin to tense. She grabbed the screwdriver once again and slowly walked toward the bedroom door. Her heart was pounding so loudly that she could barely hear anything else, and she told herself to calm down. Her nerves were simply on edge and she was just overreacting. Right?

"Julian Cooper is long gone. He won't show back up in this area again."

As Sheriff Ward's words ran through her mind, the bedroom door slowly swung open and Misty felt her entire body begin to tremble. She waited, her fingers wound tightly around the screwdriver handle. A large shadow filled the doorway, but it wasn't until the figure stepped into the light that Misty's eyes widened in surprise.

"Harris, what on earth are you doing here?" she demanded.

The young rookie cop stepped into the room, his eyes carefully taking in his surroundings. His ever-present glasses were nowhere to be seen, and something about his demeanor seemed very different.

"Don't you know why I'm here?" he asked.

Her forehead wrinkling, Misty shook her head and said, "No, I don't. Has something else happened? Where is Tori?"

Harris propped himself on the top step of the stepladder and crossed his arms, a slight smirk forming on his face. Misty had liked Harris ever since she'd first met him a couple of months ago, but there was something about him now that was setting off warning bells in her mind.

"Tori is downstairs, but she's a little tied up at the moment," he replied, a glint coming into his eyes. "I used her cellphone to text Dylan Mitchell; he'll be here in a few minutes."

"What's going on, Harris?" Misty wanted to know. "Why is Dylan on his way to my house?"

"To kill Tori."

CHAPTER 29

The screwdriver was still firmly locked between Misty's fingers as she gasped and took a small, staggering step backward. **"What?"**

Harris stared at her for a moment, the muscle in his jaw twitching. The look in his eyes was an odd mixture of warmth, anger, and something very, very dark. Misty continued to back away until she bumped into the window on the other side of the room.

"It has to be this way," he finally said. "This isn't how I originally planned it all, but it will still work. You'll see. And then you and I can be together."

Misty blinked. "What...what exactly are you saying, Harris?" she stammered.

Standing, he slowly began to circle the room. "I never intended to fall for you, Misty," he said with a slight laugh. "I came to Shady Pines for one reason and one reason only. When I saw you, though, I just couldn't believe that such beauty existed. You were so nice to me, too, but I knew you never really *saw* me."

"Misty, Misty, with hair as black as a raven's wings and eyes the color of silver. You never see me, but I see you, and I long to hold you forever."

The first note that was left on her front porch

flashed across Misty's mind, and her eyes widened. "*You* were the one leaving me those notes?" she asked.

Harris sighed. "Yes," he replied. "And now we can finally be together. After I finish what I came here to do, of course."

"And what did you come here to do?" she questioned.

"I came here to get back at Dylan Mitchell," Harris stated, his jaw clenching once more. "I didn't know exactly how I was going to do it, but when I found out what Hayden and his half-brother were up to, I decided it was the perfect set-up. We three joined forces with the promise that they could do what they wanted with the women as long as they gave me seven days and Dylan was framed for it all."

"But *why?*" Misty asked as she slowly began to edge closer to the door. "What did Dylan ever do to you?"

Harris's eyes glinted with anger at Misty's question. "Dylan Mitchell is responsible for my brother's death."

Just as Harris spat out those last words, Misty lunged toward the door. She flung it open and ran out into the dark hallway, her eyes fighting to adjust to the sudden change. Going off of memory, she turned to the right and ran toward the staircase, hoping she would remember where the steps were and not fall down them.

She could hear him coming after her. Grasping

out with her hand, Misty found the railing and launched herself down the stairs. The pounding of his feet was only inches away; she could almost feel his hot breath on her neck. Where was her Taser gun? Had she left it in her car? There was no way she could find her keys and make it to her car before he caught her.

As a million thoughts and questions flew through her mind, Misty misjudged the last step and her ankle twisted beneath her. With a gasp, she tumbled forward and hit the ground with a sickening **thud** as the screwdriver clattered loudly across the hardwood floor. Before she could get her breath back, Harris was on her, yanking her arms painfully behind her back.

"I never wanted to hurt **you,** Misty," he panted as he zip-tied her wrists together. "I even saved you when Hayden tranquilized your dog and tried kidnapping you. I love you, don't you understand that? Why are you running from me?"

Harris pulled Misty to her feet and dragged her into the living room, where Tori sat on the sofa with her hands and feet bound and eyes wide with fright. Harris had strapped tape tightly over Tori's mouth, and as he pushed Misty roughly onto the sofa beside her frightened friend, he pulled a gun from his back pocket.

"Why couldn't you have just stayed out of it?" he yelled, his eyes crazed and his face red. "I had it all planned out so perfectly!"

Misty didn't respond; her head was still

swimming from the fall she'd just taken. With a moan, Harris began to pace back and forth in front of them. After a moment, he seemed to pull himself together and checked Tori's phone.

"Dylan should be here any minute," he stated, his voice much more calm this time.

"You're going to kill Tori and blame it on Dylan?" Misty asked. "It'll just be your word against his, you know."

With a short laugh, Harris sat on the hearth and smirked at her. "Do you really think I'm that stupid?" he asked. "I'm going to take them both back to his house, kill **both** of them and make it look like a murder/suicide. I'll leave a message behind in red spray paint, just like I did at the vet, and Dylan's fingerprints will be all over both the can and the gun. I've already planted the muddy boots in his barn that match the footprints behind the hardware store, and Julian Cooper's body will be found buried on his property."

Misty's eyes widened. "You killed Julian?"

"Yes, and I also killed Hayden," he replied. "I arrived just before he fell down the steps, and when I realized he was still alive, I broke his neck. I was about to finish my plan and kill the three women and take you with me when I looked out the window and saw a police car pulling up to the asylum. I figured there were more on the way, so I got out while I could."

Misty could hardly believe her ears. She hadn't really killed Hayden? The knowledge of that fact made the burden she'd been carrying these last three days disappear. How was she going to get out of *this,* though? Harris was crazy, but he had a plan and was going to execute it no matter what; she could see it in his eyes.

Clearing her throat, Misty stated, "You won't get away with this, Harris. My security cameras are back in working order now, so the fact that you arrived at my house before Dylan has all been recorded. It will also show you dragging the three of us away from here."

"I can always erase the video footage," he snarled.

Suddenly, there was a knock at the front door. With an evil, malicious smile, Harris said, "Dylan has arrived." Raising his voice, he called out for Dylan to come inside.

Just as the front door opened, Misty turned to scream at him to run, but Harris was too quick for her. He slapped a hand across her mouth, silencing her, and she watched in horror as Dylan walked into the room, totally unsuspecting.

"Harris, what is going on?" Dylan asked when he spotted Misty and Tori on the sofa with their hands tied. He then noticed the gun Harris was holding and his eyes widened.

"Don't do it," Harris snapped as Dylan made a move for his own gun. "Slowly lower it to the floor and slide it this way."

Dylan did as Harris instructed, his face full of confusion. "Are you going to tell me what this is all about?" he wanted to know.

Harris picked up Dylan's gun and tucked his own gun into the side of his pants. Retrieving a photo from his shirt pocket, he tossed it at Dylan and asked, "Recognize the man standing on your left?"

Dylan picked up the picture and looked at it. "Yes," he replied, looking back at Harris. "He was your older brother, wasn't he?"

Misty watched as Harris blinked in surprise. "You *knew*?" he asked. "But I used my mother's maiden name."

Dylan nodded. "I do background checks on everyone who comes to work at the station, Harris. Of course, I knew. But what does your brother have to do with Misty and Tori?"

His face hard and full of disgust, Harris snarled, "You don't even care, do you? You don't care that Aaron is dead and it's *your* fault."

A look of torture passed over Dylan's face then, and he shook his head. "I didn't mean for it to happen," he told Harris. "Our battalion was notified of an assignment and we were deployed within just a few hours. Harris, your brother should never have been allowed to go on that mission. He was…"

"Don't try to blame Aaron for your mistakes," Harris ground out in anger.

Dylan raised his hands. "I'm not," he said. "But your family was never told the real story. You don't know what really happened that night."

Harris rolled his eyes. "I guess it was all Aaron's

fault?" he asked cynically. "How typical for you to blame my brother when he can't defend himself."

"Ask Colonel Johnson," Dylan stated. "He'll tell you the truth."

Harris stared at him suspiciously. "Why didn't he tell us the truth before?" he wanted to know, raising an eyebrow.

"Because I asked him not to," Dylan replied. With a sigh, he ran a hand down the side of his face, and Misty realized how exhausted he looked. He took a seat in a nearby chair and looked up at Harris with regret in his eyes. "Aaron was a good friend, Harris," he said in a low voice. "When he was killed, I thought I'd never be able to forgive myself. But as time went on and all the confusion cleared, I began to realize it wasn't really my fault. You can ask Richards or Samson; they were both there when it happened. We all had our orders, but Aaron hadn't slept in four nights when the mission began and he couldn't focus. As commander of our team, I told him to stay behind, but he wouldn't listen. When he made a wrong move and blew our cover, all four of us were nearly killed. In all the confusion, I thought that *I* was responsible."

Dylan took a deep breath and bowed his head. When he raised it again moments later, his eyes were swimming with unshed tears. "I asked Colonel Johnson to tell your family it was my fault because, in a way, I felt like it was. If I'd told the colonel that Aaron shouldn't be allowed to go on the mission in the first place, he might still be alive today."

As Dylan relayed the story, Misty thought back to the photographs she'd seen in his office, and her eyes widened as realization sunk in. The uniforms the men were wearing in those pictures had been slightly different; they were wearing tan berets. Officer Dylan Mitchell had once been an Army Ranger.

"So, then, it really **was** your fault," Harris hissed. The hate in his eyes as Dylan spoke had only grown worse, and Misty's heart leaped when he tightened his grip on Dylan's gun.

Dylan stared at Harris calmly for a moment, his eyes taking in his opponent's stance and the raised gun. Slowly, he stood to his feet and said, "If you want to kill me, Harris, then so be it. But leave Misty and Tori out of this."

"I'm afraid it's too late for that," Harris stated. "Tori is going to die tonight, and you'll be to blame for it. I've had it all planned out perfectly, and nothing is going to stop me now."

With a steely look in his eyes, Harris lowered the gun to point directly at Tori's head. She stared into the barrel with tears streaming down her cheeks, and Misty felt the breath leave her body. What should she do? If she kicked the gun, it would most likely go off anyway and kill Tori. She watched as he pulled back the hammer, her mind screaming at her to move, to do **something,** but she seemed frozen in place. Suddenly, something whizzed past her ear and struck Harris on the temple. Misty's heart nearly stopped as she waited for the gun to fire and to see her best friend fall to the floor, but nothing happened. Instead, she watched in stunned silence as Harris's eyes rolled into the back of his head and he slumped to the floor. It wasn't until then that she saw the screwdriver resting on the floor beside him.

CHAPTER 30

Tori

Two days passed, and Tori could hardly believe everything that had happened in the last two weeks. She was relieved to know that all the men involved in the kidnappings were no longer a threat, but she still couldn't believe that Harris had been the mastermind behind it all. And Hayden, her own neighbor, was a serial killer whose sole purpose in buying the house next to hers was to kidnap and kill her! It all seemed like a horrible nightmare, but at least it was finally over.

Tori was slowly trying to get back to feeling normal again, but it wasn't easy. She found herself jumping at every sound, and her nights were still restless and filled with nightmares. She wasn't ready to go home by herself just yet, so she continued staying with her parents. Her dad was still on the mend after the car accident, so she was glad to be able to help him and her mom. They'd both suffered so much the last two weeks, and Tori felt guilty for being the cause of so much pain. At least they were all beginning to heal, and she was more thankful for them now than ever.

It was Friday morning, and Tori was outside

watching her father's beautiful horses as they pranced and frolicked out in the field. With the entrance into May, the weather was starting to get warmer, and the horses were loving it. As a soft breeze ruffled Tori's curls around her face, she closed her eyes and took a deep, cleansing breath. She was just about to call out to Trampas, the gorgeous Appaloosa who was her favorite of her father's horses when her cell phone vibrated in her pocket.

"Good morning. How are you holding up?"

The text message was from her ex-boyfriend, Chris Caddel. Except for when he'd rescued her at Misty's house a few weeks ago, she hadn't seen or spoken to him since they broke up after high school. She could still remember how much in love with him she'd been, and how heartbroken she was when he'd ended things between them.

"I'm doing okay," she wrote back. *"Thanks for checking on me."*

It took a few moments for Chris to respond, and when he did, the message caught her by surprise.

"I'm so glad you're okay, Tori; I was so worried about you when I found out what happened. I've had you on my mind every day since I saw you a few weeks ago. I hadn't realized until then how much I've missed you. Would you be opposed to going out to dinner with me sometime soon?"

Tori's thumb hung suspended over the letters on her keyboard as she pondered what to say. She'd missed Chris as well. They had, after all, dated for two whole years during high school. He was her first kiss, the first boy she'd ever loved. But how did she feel about possibly rekindling their relationship? Was she crazy to even consider it after the way he broke her heart?

Before she could give him an answer, Tori was suddenly distracted when a large truck turned onto their driveway. She immediately recognized the driver and smiled in surprise, throwing up her hand in a wave.

"Good morning, Dylan," she greeted the handsome detective.

"Good morning," he said with a smile as he parked his truck and climbed out. "I hope it's okay that I stopped by so early?"

Tori nodded. "Of course. Is everything okay?"

Dylan leaned his elbows over on the fence and looked out at the horses. The morning sun glinted within his deep brown eyes, and Tori could see a small, fresh cut on his jaw where he'd cut himself shaving.

"Everything is fine," he told her, the rumble in his deep voice causing the horse's ears to flick. "Harris signed a confession last night. If he doesn't get the death penalty, he'll be in prison for the rest of his life."

Relief flooded over Tori, and she whispered a silent prayer of thanks under her breath. For the last two days, she wondered what would happen to Harris. How would she be able to sleep at night, knowing he might somehow get released and come after her and Misty again? The thought had been nagging away at her nerves, and now she finally felt like she could relax.

"That's wonderful news," she breathed. "Thank you for stopping by to tell me."

Dylan didn't say anything for a moment; he simply stared silently at the horses, as if deep in thought. He then let out a soft whistle, and Tori was surprised when Kitty came trotting over. She was normally the most shy of the horses, but when Dylan held out a handful of grass and spoke gently to her, she stepped closer and nudged his fingers.

"She normally doesn't trust strangers," Tori said, smiling as Kitty nibbled at the grass in Dylan's hand.

"I've always been good with horses," he replied, gently rubbing Kitty's soft neck. "My grandfather used to have a beautiful red roan when I was a kid. She was a great horse."

As the other horses came over to see what all the fuss was about, Tori decided to tease Dylan a bit. "I hear you're also good with a screwdriver," she stated, a twinkle in her eyes.

Dylan's lips twitched slightly. "I do what I can."

"How did you know it would work, though?" she asked seriously. "Harris was only seconds away from shooting me."

"When I first entered the room, I saw the screwdriver lying on the floor," Dylan replied. "So, while I told Harris about what happened to his brother, I sat down and eased the tool toward me with my foot. When his attention was diverted and he aimed the gun at you, I grabbed the screwdriver and threw it at his head. If the sharp side had struck him, he'd be dead right now."

"Good thing you didn't miss," Tori said.

Dylan smiled and nodded his head in agreement. "I was trained in hand-to-hand combat when I was a Ranger, and knife throwing was thankfully one of the skills I attained."

Tori tilted her head and studied Dylan's profile. "Do you miss being in the army?" she asked.

Dylan thought her question over for a moment. "Sometimes I miss the brotherhood," he finally said. "You make close bonds and friendships with those you learn to trust with your life. I don't care to go back, though. The stress was starting to get to me, especially after the accident with Aaron." Looking over at her, there was warmth in his eyes as he added, "Besides, I like Shady Pines. And the people who live here."

Tori's cheeks flushed. Was he flirting with her, or was she reading too much into his words?

Clearing her throat, she said, "Well, I'm glad you're here, Dylan. Thank you for all you did to find me, and for saving my life."

"I wish I could have found y'all sooner," he replied with a sigh. "If not for Misty, who knows what would have happened? I told Sheriff Ward I wanted to search some of the old buildings around here, but he said it was just a waste of time. Maybe from now on he'll learn to listen."

"The sheriff is new at this job," Tori said, running her fingers through Little Joe's mane. "I think he was just trying to prove he knew what was best."

Dylan nodded in agreement. After a moment, he asked, "So, when can I expect to see you at the station for more self-defense lessons?"

Tori looked at him in surprise. "You still want to keep teaching me?"

Dylan leaned one elbow on the fence and turned to look at her. "Sure. Maybe the next time someone tries to kidnap you, you'll be ready for them."

Tori shook her head and huffed. "Let's hope there won't be a next time," she retorted. "But how about tomorrow? I could come by after work."

"You're going back to work so soon?" Dylan asked, raising his eyebrows.

"Yes, I miss my coffee shop," she replied. "Now that Julian and Harris are no longer a threat, I think I'm ready to start getting my life back to normal."

"Good, I'm glad to hear that," he said. With a smile pulling at his lips and a rare, teasing glint coming into his eyes, he added, "I've been missing your special cappuccino muffins."

Tori laughed. "Then I'll bring some with me tomorrow when I come by the station for my lesson."

"Sounds good to me." Taking a step back, Dylan slapped his hands lightly against his thighs and said, "I look forward to seeing you tomorrow, Miss

Barlow."

As Tori watched him drive away, a small smile formed on her lips. Dylan was different from any man she'd ever met before, and she found herself looking forward to seeing him tomorrow, too.

Just then, she realized she'd never answered Chris. Glancing down at his message once again, she took a deep breath and typed, *"Dinner would be nice."*

She wasn't sure where any of this would lead, but being open to new possibilities was something her parents had always taught her. As she turned and walked toward the house, she breathed in the warm morning air and realized she was slowly starting to feel like her old self once again.

After breakfast, Tori received a text message from Misty. It seemed she wanted to talk to her about something, so after kissing her parents goodbye, Tori grabbed her purse and headed to her friend's house. As she pulled up beside Misty's car a few minutes later, she took note of how nice the house was looking. There was still a lot of work left to do, but Misty was quickly getting it into ship-shape.

"Good morning," Misty said when she opened the front door. "How are you doing?"

"Much better than I was," Tori told her with a smile. "How about you?"

"I'm okay," Misty replied as she linked her arm

with Tori's and led her through the house. "I'm just glad it's all over."

"Me, too." Tori stopped then and looked at her friend with wide eyes. "You know, I just realized I never thanked you for finding me in that horrible asylum," she said. "You saved my life, Misty. How can I ever thank you?"

Waving a hand in the air, Misty said, "Oh, just give me free muffins for life."

With a laugh, Tori nodded and said, "It's a deal."

As they settled down on Misty's sofa in the living room, Tori immediately asked what was up. She could tell there was something on her friend's mind, and when a tight, solemn expression filled Misty's face, she started to grow concerned.

"Right before I found out you were kidnapped, I realized I had an email from the DNA website," Misty stated. "It was a message informing me that I had a paternal match."

"Oh, Misty, that's wonderful!" she cried with excitement. When Misty didn't immediately respond, she tilted her head and asked hesitantly, "Isn't it?"

"Well, I didn't want to look at it until you were found," Misty said, absently twirling a tendril of hair around her forefinger. "I wanted you to share the moment with me, but…well…my father sort of just showed up on my doorstep a few days later."

Tori's eyes widened. "He did? How on earth did he find you?"

Chewing on her bottom lip, Misty unlocked her

phone, searched for the email, and held it up to show Tori the results. "He already knew where I lived. Tori, my father is Patrick Donovan."

Tori couldn't believe her eyes. She stared at the phone screen in complete shock, unable to comprehend what Misty had just told her. Patrick Donovan, her old school teacher and the man she'd known her entire life was Misty's father?

Moving her eyes away from the phone to stare at Misty, she asked, "Are you sure?"

Misty closed the phone and nodded. Taking a deep breath, she told Tori everything. As she relayed the story, Tori felt her heart break in two. It broke for dear, sweet Mr. Donovan, for Elena who made the mistake of believing a lie, and for Misty. Because of the mistakes made by her parents, she'd lived a life mostly without love. She'd been torn from family to family, never truly fitting in anywhere, and had to learn to survive on her own when she was just a sweet, innocent little girl. She'd never have the wonderful, carefree childhood memories that Tori cherished, and as Misty began to cry, Tori cried with her.

"What are you going to do?" Tori asked as she reached out to take her friend's hand.

Misty sighed and shook her head. "I don't know," she replied, wiping her eyes. "As I watched all the families gather around you, Anna, and Lexi, I realized how desperately I wanted that for myself. Here I have the chance to finally have a relationship with my father, Tori, and I'm scared to death. Why? What is wrong with me?"

Tori smiled softly. "Nothing is wrong with you," she assured her sweet friend. "You've been thrown a pretty major curve ball, but just think of what a lucky break this is. Your very own father is someone you already know. He lives right here in Shady Pines, and he is a beloved, well-respected man in our community. What if he was some weirdo who lived in Kalamazoo, smoked marijuana, and sold stuffed cats for a living?"

Misty stared at Tori for a moment before bursting into laughter. "Leave it to you to make me feel better," she stated as she giggled. "You're right, though. I should count my blessings instead of complaining."

With a smile, Tori patted her hand and said, "Exactly. You have a right to be nervous, though. My suggestion would be to take things slow, but let him into your life. Mr. Donovan is a good man, and ever since his wife died, he's been very lonely. I think Elena would have wanted this for you; apparently, she loved him very much."

With tears filling her eyes once again, Misty leaned forward and pulled Tori into another hug. "What would I do without you, my sweet friend?" she whispered through the tightness in her throat.

Tori squeezed her back and said, "I don't know, and I hope we never have to find out."

CHAPTER 31

After talking to Tori, Misty spent the rest of the day working on the house and pondering her friend's words. With everything that had happened in the last few weeks, she felt like she'd been run over by a train. First, there was the wild trip to Dahlonega, and then as soon as Misty got back home, her best friend was kidnapped. To make matters even more confusing, she discovered that Patrick Donovan was her real father, and then Brice confessed his true feelings for her. If things didn't calm down around here, Misty felt like she might end up being committed to a mental hospital.

As the wild train of thought ran a zigzag trail through her mind, Misty stopped herself at Brice. She hadn't told Tori what happened between them; she wasn't entirely certain herself. He'd sort of confessed his feelings, hadn't he? And then there was Adam; he'd told her he wanted to talk once everything settled down. After what happened at his parents' house when Lexi was kidnapped, however, Misty wasn't too sure she **wanted** to talk things out. Would it be awkward? Perhaps he'd even changed his mind about her.

With a sigh, Misty finally put her drill down a little after six o'clock and went downstairs to take a shower. She then fixed her hair, put on a nice dress, and headed to Patrick Donovan's house. She'd never been there before and hoped he'd be home. She also hoped he wouldn't mind a little surprise visit from his...daughter. Just thinking the word made Misty catch her breath. She was someone's daughter, and not just a government-granted daughter as she'd been so many things in the past. Patrick Donovan was her father; a living, breathing blood relative. It made Misty feel excited and anxious and nervous all at the same time.

When she pulled into Mr. Donovan's driveway, it was almost seven o'clock, and it was obvious someone was home. Taking a deep breath, Misty walked to the front door, and with a trembling finger, pressed the doorbell. It seemed to take a million years for Patrick to come to the door, and when he did, the surprise on his face was obvious.

"Misty," he said, blinking. "Are...is everything okay?"

Misty nodded. "Yes," she replied in a shaky voice. "I hope you don't mind that I stopped by?"

"Oh, of course not," he replied. Stepping back, he waved a hand inside and said, "Please, come in."

Patrick led Misty into a bit outdated but very cozy living room. There was a picture of him on the mantle, standing next to a woman, and Misty stepped closer to get a better look.

"Is this your wife?" she asked, looking over her

shoulder at Mr. Donovan.

"Yes, that's Sandra," he replied with a warm smile. "We took that almost five years ago when we went to Maine on vacation."

Misty studied the older woman for a moment, taking in her kind eyes and soft smile. Patrick had an arm draped over her shoulders, and the two looked very happy together.

"She was very beautiful," Misty said, turning to smile at Patrick.

Patrick nodded. "Yes, and her heart was even more beautiful. She was a wonderful woman." Hesitating uncertainly, he asked, "Would you like something to drink?"

Misty shook her head. "No, thank you," she replied as she took a seat on the soft and somewhat lumpy sofa.

Patrick sat across from her, and she suddenly noticed that he was wearing glasses. His salt and pepper hair was more mussed than usual, and he was obviously in need of a shave. He was dressed nice, but comfortably, in a button-down shirt, a worn sweater, and house slippers. When he shifted in his seat nervously, she realized he was waiting for her to explain this sudden, unexpected visit.

Clearing her throat, Misty leaned forward and clasped her hands together at her knees. "Now that everything has settled down and I've had some time to think," she began, "I thought I should come over and talk to you about...about everything."

Patrick nodded, studying her closely. He looked

very tired, and the way he kept rubbing his temple made Misty think he must have a headache.

"When we spoke last, you said you hoped I could forgive you," she said. Tears welled up in the back of her eyes then, and Misty stopped to swallow past the lump in her throat. "I don't know why everything worked out the way it did," she finally continued, her voice tight. "I don't know why my mother didn't give you a chance to explain before she ran away. I wish she had, but I know it wasn't your fault. And even though I was angry with you for not being completely honest with me when I first asked if you remembered Elena, I understand that, too. I was just a stranger to you then, Mr. Donovan, and you'd just lost your wife and didn't care to relive any more painful memories."

As she spoke, Misty stood up and slowly began to walk around the room. Her palms were sweaty and her voice trembled with the emotions that warred within her. She was rambling, but she couldn't seem to stop herself. Her brain was flying wildly in all directions, but she tried her best to say what was in her heart.

"I guess what I'm trying to say, Mr. Donovan, is that I do forgive you," she said, turning to face him. "I...I don't know exactly where to go from here, but if you're willing, I'd like to remain good friends and maybe...maybe one day we'll start to feel like father and daughter."

Tears were trickling down Patrick's cheeks as he stood up and gently took one of Misty's hands. "I think that's a wonderful idea," he said in a choked voice. "And thank you, Misty, for giving me a chance."

Misty nodded, and when Patrick said he wanted to give her something, she sat back down and waited as he left the room. When he returned moments later, he was carrying a small box.

"Sandra never knew about this," he said as he sat next to her and carefully opened the old container. "But I've kept it all these years."

With a trembling hand, he pulled out an old photograph of himself sitting next to Elena. It appeared they were on a picnic, and their arms were wrapped around each other, and they looked so happy. Misty smiled as she looked into her mother's beautiful eyes, wishing once again that she could have known her.

"I kept this, too," Patrick said, and Misty watched as he pulled a beautiful sapphire ring from the box. It glittered in the light, and when Misty took a closer look, she saw the letters "P&E" engraved on the side.

"This is the engagement ring I had made for your mother," he said, sniffing as he handed it to her. "Misty, I'd like you to have it."

Her eyes widening, Misty looked up at him and said, "Oh, I couldn't…"

"Please," he interrupted, holding up a hand. "I want you to have it. She would want that, too."

Pulling her locket from around her neck, Misty opened it for a moment and looked at the picture inside. For so many years, this tiny photograph was all she'd had of her mother, and now she had so much more. Snapping the locket closed, Misty attached the ring to the chain and pressed both the ring and locket against her heart.

"Thank you, Mr. Donovan," she said with a warm smile that was filled with so many emotions. "I'll cherish it forever."

Mr. Donovan asked her to stay for supper, as he hadn't eaten yet. Misty agreed, and while they ate, they talked about Elena. Or rather, Patrick talked and Misty happily listened. He told her so many things about her mother, and once they were finished eating, he told her more. He said that Elena would never share much about her childhood, but she was from Cuba and had two sisters. When she was eight, her mother put her on a boat and sent her to America to live with her aunt.

"Her father had just died, and Elena's mother wanted a better life for her daughter," Patrick said. "Elena's two sisters stayed behind because they were too young to make the journey. Two years later, Elena's aunt died, and she was put into foster care."

Misty could hardly believe her ears. Her mother had also been raised in the foster system? How horrible it must have been for her to know she had a family back home, a mother and two sisters, but was unable to get back to them.

"Did she keep in touch with her family in Cuba?"

Misty asked. "Did she ever see them again?"

Patrick shook his head. "She lost contact with them after her aunt died," he said. "She tried to find them again after she turned eighteen, but they had disappeared. She never knew what happened to them, and it broke her heart. During one of the rare times when she would talk about them, she said when she left Cuba, she was too young to understand that she'd probably never see her mother and sisters again. Once she was in America and came to realize what was happening, she had nightmares for weeks. She said her aunt was the only light in all of that darkness, and after she was gone, Elena knew she was truly alone."

Tears filled Misty's eyes, and she reached up to wipe her cheeks. "One of her friends in Dahlonega said she was often mistreated because of her ethnicity."

Taking a deep breath, Patrick nodded and said, "I think she may have also been mistreated in her foster homes. She refused to talk about it and would change the subject any time I brought it up."

Misty closed her eyes for a moment, her heart hurting at everything her mother had to endure in her short lifetime. At least, even if just for a little while, she'd known and experienced true love, and Misty found comfort in that knowledge.

She stayed at Mr. Donovan's house for a while longer, and when she left, he asked her to come again soon.

"There's always more I can share about Elena,"

he told her, "and I want to show you pictures of your grandparents. They're both gone now, but they contacted me after I'd been married for nearly three years and we managed to patch things up. I also have a sister who lives in Pennsylvania with her husband and two sons. So, I'd love to share everything I can with you about my family, because they're your family, too."

Misty promised she'd see him soon, and as she backed out of his driveway and drove away, it felt as if a missing piece of her heart had finally found its way home.

CHAPTER 32

The next day, Misty practiced in her mind what she would say to Brice when she went to see him. The hardware store had re-opened a couple of days before, which meant Brice was working and wouldn't be home until later in the evening.

Butterflies danced in her stomach all day long. What should she wear? Should she just blurt everything out right up front, or let him speak first? What if she couldn't say what was in her heart and ended up making a fool of herself?

It was just after five o'clock, and Misty was on her back porch, installing a new light. Since she lived pretty far outside of town and the trees surrounding her house were so tall, it could get mighty dark out there at night. So, she'd ordered a new, brighter light and decided that once she was finished installing it, she'd take a shower and head on over to Brice's house.

Misty's phone sat on the railing and was loudly playing old Nat King Cole classics. Nat's soothing voice was helping to calm her nerves, and as Wally was inside and not around to alert her to company, she failed to hear the sound of an approaching vehicle. She was so engrossed in her work that she didn't see the large figure of a man walking around the house toward her. When a deep voice suddenly spoke out from behind, her nerves were so on edge that she dropped her drill and shrieked in terror. Jerking around, her foot slipped from the top rung of the step ladder, and with flailing arms, she fell on her rear end with a painful *thud.*

"Misty, are you alright?"

Strong hands grabbed her under the arms and hoisted her to her feet. Stars bounced before her eyes as Misty stared up at Brice, and the look of concern on his face would have been endearing if he hadn't just tried to kill her.

"Are you trying to get rid of me or what?" Misty mumbled as she rubbed her jarred head.

"I'm sorry, Misty. I thought you heard me coming," he replied. "You didn't break anything, did you?"

With a frown, Misty walked around the porch for a moment, her backside aching. Finally, she turned to him and said, "I might not be able to sit for a few days, but I don't think anything is broken."

His lips twitching slightly, Brice said, "Consider this payback for the first time we met."

Unable to stop herself, Misty burst into laughter. She could still see him at the bottom of that ladder in Barlow's Hardware Store with what looked like a million nails scattered all over the floor. She hadn't been watching where she was going and had run right into him with her buggy.

"I believe you compared me to a thoroughbred in the Kentucky Derby," she stated, still chuckling.

Brice raised an eyebrow, his blue eyes twinkling mischievously. "Was I wrong, though?"

Misty grabbed a nearby hammer and acted like she was going to throw it at him. "Watch it, Barlow," she told him as he ducked out of the way, and they both laughed. Putting the hammer back down, she asked, "So, to what do I owe the pleasure of this visit?"

Turning serious, Brice stuffed his hands into his pockets and said, "I wanted to see you. It's been over a week since we...well, since we last spoke, and I thought maybe we could talk things over."

Misty's heart immediately kicked into overdrive at his words. Clearing her throat, she nodded and said, "Okay. Would you like to come inside?"

Brice looked around the spacious back porch and shook his head. "If it's okay with you, I wouldn't mind staying out here," he said. "The weather is so nice, and I like listening to the sound of the wind as it blows through the pine trees. It's very soothing."

"I like it, too," Misty replied with a smile. Leaning against the porch railing, she crossed her arms and just looked at him, waiting. He walked slowly around the porch for a moment, not saying a word, and she anxiously wondered what he had to say.

"Now that things have settled down," he finally began, "I'd like to start by apologizing for the way I acted last week."

Oh boy, here we go, Misty thought with an inward groan. ***He's sorry for kissing me and for the things he said.***

"Instead of calmly telling you how I feel," he continued, "I got too upset and acted badly."

With a sigh, he pushed his hands into his pockets and looked out over the yard for a moment, as if trying to gather his thoughts. Misty remained silent, her stomach in knots as she wondered where all of this was going.

Turning back to look at her, Brice said, "I know you and Adam had a…thing before you found out that Elena's husband wasn't your real father. So, when you told me you were with him all day, I… well, I guess I just got jealous."

Misty blinked and raised her eyebrows, feeling a little surprised at Brice's words. She hadn't been able to tell if he was jealous or simply overreacting about everything because of Tori.

Stepping closer, Brice rested a hand on the railing next to Misty and asked, "Do you remember when I ran into your house and told you that Tori had just been kidnapped?" When Misty nodded, he continued, "I was coming over to talk to you about what happened in Dahlonega. I'd spoken to Tori and told her I was apprehensive about getting involved with you."

Her forehead wrinkling, Misty tilted her head and asked, "Why is that?"

Brice shook his head and looked down at the boards beneath their feet, but not before Misty saw what looked to be pain in his eyes.

"After everything I've been through with my dad's death, my mom and her...well, her issues, and then my fiancé running off with my best friend, I just don't trust easily anymore." Looking back up at her, he continued, "And I know how life has been for you, Misty. You've never stayed in one place for long, and I guess I was just afraid you'd eventually get tired of Shady Pines **and** me and decide to leave."

Misty reached out and took his hand, her heart breaking just a little. She knew what he'd been through; she'd suffered from similar experiences and knew how it affected one's outlook on life. For once, though, he was being completely open and honest about his feelings, and the butterflies in her stomach grew even stronger.

"I'm not going anywhere, Brice," she said softly.

He stared at her for a moment, his beautiful, soulful eyes searching hers. There was electricity between them, a connection Misty felt so strongly that it was all she could do not to lean closer to him. There was something else he needed to say, though; she could see it on his face, and so she waited. In a moment, a soft smile spread across his face and he gently squeezed her hand.

"You know, I felt a connection with you the first day we met," he said as he looked deeply into her eyes, "but I was too afraid of getting into another relationship. If you'll have me now, though, I'm more than ready and willing to give it a try. I've fallen in love with you, Misty Raven, and I don't want to lose you."

Smiling softly, Misty fought back the tears and emotions that flooded over her at his words. In all her life, she'd never felt the way she did in this moment. She felt safe, secure, and truly loved, and like she'd finally found a piece of herself that she'd always been missing.

"I love you, too," she said in a choked voice. Her eyes began to twinkle then, and she stepped closer and said, "In fact, I was planning to go to your house tonight to tell you just that."

His eyes widening in surprise, Brice raised his eyebrows and asked, "You mean I could have saved myself all this stress if I'd just gone straight home and waited?"

Laughing, Misty stood on her tip-toes and slowly wrapped her arms around his neck. With a grin, she said, "That's right, but I sure enjoyed hearing what you had to say."

The look in Brice's eyes made her heart catch as he leaned in closer. "And I enjoyed saying it," he whispered, just before capturing her lips with his own.

They stood there on her back porch, lost in their embrace, and Misty knew that another part of the puzzle had clicked into place. As she relished the warmth of Brice's strong arms and listened to the wind as it whispered through the pine trees, she knew she really was home.

EPILOGUE

4 months later

Misty stared up at her house as excitement coursed through her body. It was finished. After a whole year, the house renovations were finally finished. And what a year it had been!

She looked around at the people there to help her celebrate, and warmth filled her heart. All the Barlows were there, of course, along with Dylan Mitchell, Kyra Kirby, and her boyfriend, Samuel. Chris Caddel and his grandfather, Joe, had also shown up, and Misty smiled as she watched Dylan and Chris crowd in next to Tori.

And then there was her father. During the last four months, she and Patrick had grown closer as they explored their newfound father-daughter relationship. They ate supper together at least twice a week, and he'd come by the house many times to help her with the renovations. He'd given her a whole photo album that was filled with pictures of her grandparents and had shared dozens of stories about them. She knew he still struggled with guilt over everything that had happened between him and his parents when he was young, but she was so glad they'd eventually patched things up. He'd loved his parents a great deal; she could hear it in his voice and see it on his face anytime he spoke of them. He gave Misty a quilt his mother made and a pocket watch that belonged to his dad. Misty soaked it all in and wished she could have known them, but in a way, she felt as if she did through all of Patrick's stories.

Patrick's older sister, Lola Cambridge, had also come for a surprise visit with her husband and two sons. Misty could hardly believe she had five family members now. The Cambridge's were such nice people, too, and Misty couldn't wait to get to know them better.

Stepping up onto the front porch, Misty declared to everyone that she'd like to say something. They all quieted down and turned to face her, and with a smile, she said, "I'd like to thank you all for coming out today, and also for helping me so much around the house these last four months. If not for you, it wouldn't be ready for its grand opening next weekend. I never thought I'd open a bed-and-breakfast. In fact, I wasn't sure I'd ever settle down anywhere, but I'm so thankful I've found such a wonderful place." Smiling warmly at them all, she added, "And such a wonderful family."

With lots of smiles and cheers, everyone gave her a hug or high-five as they filed inside to eat cake and ice cream. Tori pulled Misty into a warm embrace, and when she leaned back a moment later, her eyes were swimming as she said, "I'm so thankful you're part of our family, too."

Brice was the last in line, and once everyone was inside, he gently cupped her chin and bent down to kiss her. Misty wrapped her arms snugly around his waist and sighed inwardly. She'd never dreamed she could be so happy. After her talk with Brice four months ago, she'd spoken to Adam and told him what was in her heart. He'd been hurt at first but eventually came around; he'd even done some last-minute electrical work on the house for her. He was a good man, and Misty hoped he'd find happiness with someone someday.

"Well, Miss Raven, are you ready for all the many adventures to come when the *Shady Pines Inn* opens next week?" Brice asked as he took her hand.

Misty laughed. "Oh, I'm sure I can handle it." Her eyes twinkling, she added, "With your help, of course."

They walked toward the front door and Misty turned to look back at her custom-made wooden sign that stood proudly at the end of her driveway. As it swayed softly in the wind, she couldn't help but wonder just what sort of adventures the future really did hold.

A NOTE FROM THE AUTHOR:

Thank you so much for reading book #4 of "A Shady Pines Mystery" series. If you enjoyed it, please leave a review on Amazon or Goodreads – or both! Reviews really help! I look forward to hearing from you. Also, if you're interested in receiving news of upcoming books, discounts, free e-books, and more, please sign up for my newsletter at:

newsletter.jennyelaineauthor.com

www.ingramcontent.com/pod-product-compliance
Lightning Source LLC
Chambersburg PA
CBHW032029310726
48972CB00002B/594